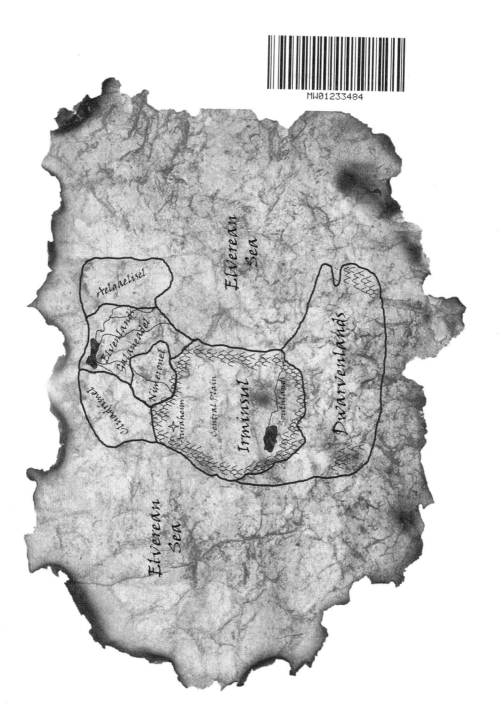

SWORD DREAMER

Marshal Myers (signature)

MARSHAL MYERS

electricmoon
publishing

Visit us at www.emoonpublishing.com

This book is dedicated to
My God, for giving me the gift of writing.
My Mom, for being an indefatigable editor.
Jeff Dunn for being the catalyst of the revolution in me
that led to this book.
And to my best friend Ben, for introducing me to
the wonderful world of High Fantasy.

ONE

A SLEEPER LIES DREAMING

The Red Griffin was filled with the usual local shady customers that frequented the inns of southern Irminsul. Country haunts of its type were always filled with highway bandits, cutthroats, and pickpockets. Several honest farmers would occasionally drop in for a draught as well, but these honest men typically made no conversation with the rogues who shared their grease-stained tables.

The inn was built on a small knoll overlooking the village of Brimaug in the pastoral Southlands of the kingdom of Irminsul. This "village" was nothing more than a hodgepodge of hastily built houses with thatched roofs of dirty straw, thrown together around a muddy track of land which served as a crude marketplace. Not far beyond the inn was a small forest beyond which tiny farms were scattered here and there. It was from these farms that The Red Griffin obtained its supply of food, though the farmers were often cheated, as the keeper of the house was a coin pincher who always paid the lowest possible price for everything in his weather-beaten establishment, resulting in fare of meager quality.

Most of the inns of the pastoral Southlands of Irminsul were shoddily built, and The Red Griffin was no exception. The windowless tavern had been built of young, unhardened yew wood, now darkened by many years of flowing pipe smoke, smoke which was so thick it made breathing extremely difficult. The thatched roof leaked when it rained, contributing even more to the musty smell inside the inn. There was a small fireplace where logs, which were kept meticulously dry despite the damp climate by being concealed in dirty wool blankets, crackled and provided the heat with which to cook meager suppers. One such meal was a nauseating yellow vegetable concoction with indiscernible chunks of meat and tripe. The innkeeper, a fat old bald man with a bulbous nose who wore a grease-stained apron, designated this stomach-turning slop to be a stew, the finest meal the house had to offer. A wooden counter lined with stools stood in front of the fire. On the front of this counter was carved a winged griffin, the red paint having long ago chipped away from its beaked head, talons and powerful feline legs. A tankard cabinet stood a few feet behind the counter. This was lined with wooden pints, as the keeper of the house could not afford mugs made of tin. A few feet behind the stools were four heavy long tables lined with benches, which were stained with ale.

It was late at night, and the usual crowd of ruffians was already half-intoxicated. These men were unshaven, unkempt and filthy, wearing dirty patched trousers and shirts, with hands always twitching towards the handles of their knives.

They generally busied themselves with their own devilish schemes, as news of the war to the north seldom reached the rural southern lands. Yet the general country folk did not remain entirely aloof from politics. They knew of the rebellion near the cities of the North from minstrels, travelers and merchants who came down to earn money or participate in country fairs and bazaars. They did not care who ruled Irminsul. They simply minded their own business and distanced themselves from northern "foreigners". Most of the country folk were illiterate. All of the schools and places of study were in the cities of the North, the most famous one being in Auraheim, the capital city of Irminsul. That city stood at the base of the northern portion of the Kjarten Mountains, which encircled the country of Irminsul, giving it its ring shape. The northern portion of the country was separated from the southern portion by a broad, golden grassy plain which was dotted with forests. People seldom went through these forests, as many of them were said to not only be filled with vicious beasts, but also haunted by malevolent spirits.

The great door of the inn creaked open and shut, and two tall strangers, wrapped entirely in tattered, mud-stained cloaks, their faces almost completely concealed by large hoods, walked quietly into the room. They kept their entire persons concealed within their cloaks and they bore themselves in a secretive manner, yet no one could help noticing their tall, commanding presence. Two men sitting in a corner throwing dice looked up suspiciously, weighing the odds of good results coming from roughing the newcomers, as the strangers passed. The tall strangers sat down at the bar away from the other customers. The innkeeper squinted one eye, trying to recognize the hidden faces. Not only could he not see or recognize them, but his eyes were poor from years of working before a roaring fire, so he gave up the fruitless endeavor and merely prepared to serve them. What kind of men they were, or more importantly, how well they paid, he could not tell.

The one on the left was of slightly more powerful build than his companion, though in height he was a few inches shorter. He whispered in a commanding voice, "Innkeeper, two ales and bowls of stew." The innkeeper caught a glint of gold as the stranger reached into a hidden purse. A dozen gold coins jingled on the counter, and set for a moment, glistening in the firelight. The innkeeper's eyes glistened in return. He, normally a very rude man, immediately became extremely polite.

"Will you be wanting anything else, good sir?"

"No thank you."

The speaker's face was still concealed, yet the end of a fiery red beard was visible.

"You have a northern sound to your tongue," remarked the innkeeper. "Who are you?"

"I am no one to be trifled with," came the quick, biting answer.

"Will you require a room for the night?"

"No. I must leave soon."

"What of your companion? Has he not the powers of speech?"

"He speaks when he has something to say. Leave him be."

"Will he stay the night?"

"No. He goes with me."

One of the intoxicated blackguards had been keeping his wandering eye as best as he could on the powerful stranger, for ruffians of his kind were always suspicious of outsiders. He laid his groping hands on the table and pushed himself up to a shaky standing position. He staggered over to the bar, his legs scissoring and knocking over furniture as he came. He plopped, slumping, down on the stool to the left of the traveler and slouched towards him. Taking blurry note of the tip of the red beard, he said in a slurred voice, "Aha, I know who you are."

He fumbled for his knife. "Gollmorn's gonna pay good for your hide!"

In the blink of an eye, before the drunk had a chance to strike, the stranger whirled on the stool and stood to his full height, shedding his cloak. He was a red-bearded giant, clad in a fine hauberk. His blue eyes flared like hot steel with anger, and his long fiery locks fell almost to his shoulders. He whipped out his massive broadsword from the leather baldric on his back, and pointed the tip of the broad blade at the would-be assassin's breast. He then seized the bewildered, hazy-eyed man by the throat in a vice grip and, in a feat of almost superhuman strength, hurled the brute across the room. There was a great thud as his mangy head hit the wall, and immediately his ale-stained dinner gurgled up out of his grease-ridden mouth as he sank into a stinking heap.

Everyone in the room gasped, staring in the direction of the counter. It was not so much at the display, even though the man was apparently a soldier, for there had been bloody brawls in The Red Griffin before. When he looked up from the sorry heap of humanity that he had just rendered unconscious, the soldier followed everyone's shocked gaze. He looked over at his companion, and saw to his dismay that he had also shed his cloak. His unusually tall stature, long hair and pointed ears betrayed him to be an elf, such as the ones who used to come on dragons and, very rarely, flying unicorns south from their home north of the northern Kjartens to serve as mercenaries in the Army of the King before the civil war. His dark eyes and ebon mane and skin gave him a look of majesty. He also wore a hauberk over which he wore a bright blue surcoat with no emblem. A large crossbow was in his left hand and a large scimitar hung at his waist, both of which had been hidden by his oversized cloak.

The red-haired warrior took out his bulging purse and emptied it onto the counter. The whirring sound of the gold as it hit the counter and its glittering sheen caused most of the ruffians to purge what they had just seen from their memories. Their avarice was greater than their sense of honesty or duty to the law. The corrupt village sheriff was there that night and decided to let the incident pass unpunished in order to gain the profit that he guessed was soon in coming.

"Let each man take his share, even the one against the wall," the red-bearded swordsman said gravely. He scanned every face threateningly. "Not a word of this to anyone."

He took the elf by the arm and led him out of the tavern. As they walked through the door he whispered, "Do not worry, my friend. Things will be better once we find the Sword Dreamer."

Léofric lay fast asleep on a pile of hay in the barn of his mother's farm. The sun beamed through the hole in the thatched roof and the light danced on his handsome face. The barn was a long oblong structure built of oaken planks with rafters that reached up about twelve feet above the ground, giving the roof a slightly prismatic shape. On the right side were three wooden stalls for the cow, the goat, and the mule. A hen roost was built up near the rafters, and the pullets squawked and fluttered from time to time.

It had been Léofric's habit to nap in the barn since he was a small boy, and he was now a strapping lad of eighteen. For as long as he could remember, he had always had strange dreams while sleeping in the hay. These inexplicable dreams were becoming stranger still, and he was now completely immersed in one of them.

As he lay there, his face would twitch with the excitement of what he saw in his mind. His subconscious eyes were completely focused. He dreamed of mail-clad warriors, paladins of the King, charging downhill to meet the enemy below. In his mind's eye, the sun glinted on steel as the mighty hosts clashed. In his dreams, he always saw the enemy's movements and plan of attack first. Then, as if by some mysterious supernatural aid, the Army of King Futhark of Irminsul would strike as though it had foresight into the enemy's exact thoughts and strategies.

Today in Léofric's dream, the two great hosts were on the brink of clashing when a harsh yet loving voice broke through Léofric's subconscious.

"Léofric. Léofric, my son. Wake up. Your chores are waiting. It would not be well for you to lie here all day. Come now, open your eyes."

Léofric's eyes fluttered open and he saw his mother, Ragna, looking down at him, shaking her flaxen head. A slight smile turned her lips. Her blue eyes were alive with amusement. She was in her late thirties, yet still clinging to the beauty of her youth. In her younger days she had been spry, strikingly beautiful and full of good cheer. But a shadow had fallen on her countenance just before her son was born. Yes, she laughed and was merry many times, but there was a void in her heart that not even Léofric could fill, a void the source of which he could never quite discern.

"Léofric, you must do your chores now."

"Yes, mother." He jumped up and leaned down to kiss her cheek, for he towered a full foot above her.

Léofric first went down to the small pond that lay in the center of their property to retrieve water for the animals in the stalls. It was early in the spring, and the grass grew fertile and green. Léofric looked at his reflection in the pond. He was a strong, tall, handsome youth with sea-blue eyes and golden red hair. His muscles were corded from years of farm work. On many hot summer days, he would run across the hills of the countryside and swim in the pond for hours, which contributed all the more to his strength, quickness and agility.

He did not have any friends in the surrounding villages, for they believed him to be strange for dreaming of being a warrior. Therefore, he had learned not to share his dreams of battle with anyone for fear of being ridiculed. There seemed to be no place, even with the love of his mother, where he truly belonged. He fell like a stranger, an outcast, without friends or solace.

He also had no interest in any of the girls in the surrounding district, pretty though they were. It was strange, for in addition to dreams of battle he was now dreaming of a tall girl with long black hair and ebon skin. In his dreams, the girl seemed to be beckoning for him to follow her, but he never had the chance before he awoke and she was gone. He could not determine the cause of these dreams.

His mother constantly worried about him. She discouraged his dream of being a fighter, as she was very anxious for his safety, for which reason Léofric thought her overbearing at times.

Léofric never knew his father and his mother never spoke of him, so Léofric knew not if he was living or dead. Léofric had never asked his mother about his father directly, as his mother made clear by her attitude whenever he hinted at the subject that doing so was taboo. Very often however, Léofric would hear her crying softly to herself in the middle of the night and surmise that she was thinking of her lost husband.

Léofric did not care for farm work, but did his best in everything in order to please his mother. The one true, loving friend and faithful confidant was Luath, the dun cow. He spoke to her as he milked her and she chewed grass slowly and thoughtfully. He would tell her the things that he dared not tell anyone else, and she would simply look back as though she were some mystic, elderly sage.

"Maybe someday I will meet my father," he would say enthusiastically. "Mayhap he is a soldier in Futhark's Army. He may come back someday and take me away to war. Then we would come back in honor and glory to mother, and we would not need you anymore. But we would not sell you to a butcher. Oh, no! You would be the most famous cow in all of the Southlands. We would buy you a silver manger for your feed. Mother does not like my talking of swords and battles, but I would be a valiant warrior, and you would be proud. I wonder if I will ever meet the mysterious dark girl who has been coming to me in my dreams. Do you think she is kind and loving, like Mother?" Luath continued to chew her cud and swat the nagging flys with her long coarse tail.

Léofric's other duties also included feeding the chickens, goat and mule. He never talked to these animals for he knew they were too stupid. He also plowed and sowed crops in the field in planting season and chopped firewood to store up during the winter months. Though he loved his mother, Luath, and the farm, truly, in his heart, Léofric desired something more than farm life, something adventurous and exciting.

He would lie on his cot night after night, month after month, hoping that the chance for adventure would come before he was too old to answer the call, and would eventually fall asleep despairingly, thinking that his insignificant, mundane life would never change. He would never find anyone whom he could love and to whom he could pour out his heart. He was a misfit, an outcast without a purpose who could never find adventure in his boring, lackluster world. Little did he know that, outside his sheltered world, events were unfolding that would provide him with an adventure greater than any even he could imagine.

TWO

THE MYSTERIOUS WARRIORS

Léofric's home was a small structure with a foundation of weather-beaten stone. This stone also accounted for the first foot of its construction. From that point upward, however, the walls were built of old, sturdy yew. The roof was thatched of good country straw, which never leaked, for Léofric was always re-thatching it in autumn to keep out the cold winds of winter and the spontaneous showers of spring. A stout stone chimney poked its head out of the left side of the roof, and during the winter months it steadily breathed forth smoke like a dragon of the mysterious Elvenlands which lay to the north of the northern Kjartens, the mountains that formed the northern border of Irminsul.

The house in which Léofric and his mother lived consisted only of three rooms: a large kitchen, Léofric's room, and his mother's room. The kitchen was a large rectangular room which was sparsely furnished. A long counter ran along the right wall. Ragna made use of this long board by preparing meals for cooking. On the left side of the room was a fairly well-sized fireplace. All of the cooking and stewing took place here, and it was here that Ragna had told him stories during the long winter nights when he was a small boy. During the spring, fall and summer, the board of fair consisted mainly of a light soup made from vegetables grown in the garden. During the winter months, however, they were fed with whatever kill Léofric could bring back from the hunt. Meals were served on the simple, rectangular wooden table in the center of the room with two wooden benches on either side. This table was not their most prized possession, lacking the flourishes and many ornate linear designs of fine craftsmanship, but it served its purpose well.

Léofric's room was small, containing only two furnishings: Léofric's cot and a short stool of oak. The straw-stuffed wool mattress that lay on the cot was covered by a deerskin in spring and summer and by the hide of a black bear in fall and winter. It had been the shining moment of Léofric's early adolescence when he had struggled through the door of the house, bearing that furry giant's carcass. His mother was loud in her praise and they had feasted heartily on bear steak for weeks.

Léofric's mother's room adjoined his room. The solitary furnishing it possessed was a huge featherbed in which Ragna slept. Often when he was a small child, Léofric would scamper into the room on stormy nights and his mother would console him. But when he began to grow older, for some strange reason, she forbade him to ever enter the room again. He began to imagine that the featherbed, which they certainly could not afford, had been a wedding present from his father. This added only more to Léofric's growing desire to discover who his father was. As the early spring of his eighteenth year progressed, his mother withdrew more and more into herself. Léofric desired to speak with her of her pensive behavior, but could never find the right occasion or the words.

One evening about a week after his mother found him in the barn, as one of the early spring's golden setting suns bathed the kitchen in fiery light, Léofric noticed that his mother was even more withdrawn than usual. As she laid the porridge on the supper table and turned back for the barley bread, he noticed her wipe a solitary tear from her cheek. She said very little during dinner and after the table was cleared went straightaway to her room, which was the largest room in the small, three-room house,. Léofric sighed, shook his head and prepared for bed, the image of his wistful mother ever in the forefront of his mind.

Léofric tossed and turned in his bed that night. His stomach was churning and he broke into a cold sweat. He sensed in his heart that a great change was coming, a dramatic change the manner of which he could not guess. At the midnight hour, still unable to sleep, his ears alerted to a sound, a whimpering sound, stifled like that of a dog. He realized that it was his mother crying. Then he resolved to do something the next morning that he had never dared to do: he would ask his mother directly about his father.

The next morning, as his mother was clearing away the leftover bread and cheese, Léofric cleared his throat and asked, "Mother, may I speak with you? I have a request I must ask of you."

Ragna laid the breadboard down, and turned to look at him. "Certainly, my son. What is it?"

Léofric laid a gentle hand on her arm. "Mother, I know this is very painful for you, but I think I am now of an age to know."

He could see a worried expression fill her countenance. He looked intently into her eyes. "Please, tell me who my father is."

Her hand shot to her mouth, her eyes widened, and a tear ran down her cheek. "You must not ask me these things. You must never know."

Léofric could not understand how his mother could profess to love him and yet keep such secrets from him. Becoming frustrated, he demanded, "And why not? He is my father, after all. I have been ridiculed and looked down upon by the lads of the village long enough."

"You must never speak of this again," she commanded, shouting and striking the table with her fist, causing the wooden bowls to rattle.

Léofric's eyes flared like heated steel. "You probably drove him away with your infernal obstinance." So saying, he rose. Turning on his heel and seizing his small hunting bow from a peg in the wall, he stormed out of the house.

His head throbbed with anger and resounded as if it were being struck like a blacksmith's hammer on an anvil. He stalked toward the small woods that separated his farm from the nearest village. Often he would go there to think or calm down when he needed a place to be alone. He would walk beneath the tall, ivy and moss-covered trees, feeling almost a kinship with the birds that sang sweetly in the trees. The damp crunch of the leaves under his booted feet would seem a symphony to him.

When his anger had cooled somewhat and his mind had turned to other matters, he thought that it would be practical to bring home a deer for supper, to help him make peace with his mother. So he treaded softly, hiding behind the trees as he went, looking for a doe or a buck, which were plentiful in that forest. Venison also happened to be one of his favorite dishes, a treat he would normally enjoy at the yearly village fair or on his birthday.

After a time, he came upon a full-grown doe, with much meat on her, standing among the roots of two close-growing trees. His mouth began to water as he saw her and thought of the meat such a kill would provide. He held his breath, knelt behind a tall oak and slowly drew out a flint-tipped arrow from the quiver on his back. He fit it to the bow and pulled back the bowstring. Just as he was about to release the arrow, the deer took fright and sprang away. Léofric sensed someone approaching softly behind him.

He whirled, arrow still pulled back tightly. Several paces back stood two tall strangers clad in mud-stained cloaks. They were leading three stallions, one black, one gray, and a younger one with a chestnut hide. One of the strangers raised a hand in greeting. Léofric had heard of bandits with hideouts in the many forests of the Southlands. Many of them would capture innocent travelers and take them to the north to sell them as slaves in some of the northern cities. There was nothing in their appearances that indicated to Léofric that this was not the case.

"Good day to you, boy."

"You are a stranger. We do not care much for strangers here. Who are you, and what business do you have in this part of the forest?" Léofric demanded.

"First give me your name. Then I will give you mine. I am a friend, though you know me not, and I am here on honorable business."

Even though Léofric felt no fear, he was still suspicious of these strangers and took the precaution of tightening his grip on his bow. "I am called Léofric."

"Who is your father?"

This tugged at a sensitive cord. Without thinking, Léofric forgot common sense and rashly responded, "I-I know not."

"And who is your mother?"

This gave Léofric a chance for a little fun. The anger in his heart was still hot enough for him to plot against those who might harm him.

He guessed that these men may be bandits. He did not want to be robbed. A plan quickly formed in his head. He would lead these men in the other direction, double-cross them and shoot them before they had a chance to do him any harm, taking the spoils of victory home to his mother, who also despised ruffians of their kind.

"My mother is called Ragna. We live in the homestead just east of these woods."

The stranger's response was quite unexpected. He threw up his hands and laughed merrily. "No you do not, liar. But anyhow, how is your mother?"

"Why do you ask?" Léofric asked warily. This man must know something that Léofric did not. Why should a bandit care how his mother fared?

Neither of the strangers answered, but instead threw back their cloaks. The speaker was a tall man of gigantic and powerful proportions. He had a long fiery mane and beard and eyes as sea-blue as Léofric's. He was clad in a fine hauberk and a massive broadsword hung from a baldric on his back. His companion was even more astonishing. He was extremely tall, much taller than the red-bearded man, and his skin and hair were as black as ebony. His long hair and pointed ears indicated what the astonished Léofric guessed: he was an elf. His kind was never seen in the Southlands, and the ignorant country folk were suspicious of their language, wisdom, and magic. He also was clad in mail over which he wore a plain, bright blue surcoat. A large crossbow hung on his back and a large scimitar was at his waist. His brown eyes betrayed wisdom and intelligence.

"Do you think your flimsy arrow could penetrate this?" The red man asked, laughing.

"Who-who are you?" Léofric stammered in bewilderment. Regaining his composure he said, "I am not afraid of you. Mail or no mail, I will send you back to your den with an arrow to tell the tale."

The red-bearded giant smiled sympathetically. "That is the right spirit, lad. I am Wulf, a soldier in Futhark's Army."

The dark elf spoke. His voice boomed like the beating of a kettle drum. "And I am Surgessar of Nilmeronel in the Elvenlands, his brother-in-arms."

Wulf said, "Now that you know us, you need to know our purpose for speaking to you. We have come to take you, Léofric, away to the war with us."

Léofric's heart leaped at the thought. He had heard of the rebellion, and the desperate struggle of the Army of King Futhark against the rebel forces. This news had only been jumbled country chatter. But, if there was truly a war, there was battle glory to be gained. Here was his chance. Yet, part of his mind was irresolute. How could he trust these men whom he did not know?

"Why should I trust you?" The boy asked. "How do I know that you will not sell me as a slave in some northern city? Strangers are known to do that around these parts."

The soldier drew his sword and held it out in front of him with the blade pointed downward. The massive broadsword was about five feet long with a shining, broad blade and a two-handed grip wrapped in wine-red leather. The fittings were steel, and the semi-cylindrical pommel ran down an inch or two from the grip in an almost teardrop shape. The quillions sloped down in a semicircular shape from the grip. The soldier's hands seemed big enough and strong enough to wield the sword with either one or two hands.

The man raised one hand in the taking of an oath. "By this blade, I swear that my intentions are honorable."

Sheathing it, he said, "What is more, Léofric, I knew your father. I swear also by that good man that you shall be safe."

Léofric's jaw dropped and he stared wide-eyed at the man, unable to speak.

"Yes," Wulf said, knowingly, "I knew your father. Moreover, I know why you dream of swords and battles. There is a reason for your desire to be a warrior. Come with me and discover it."

"A power beyond reckoning is yours," the elf said sapiently. "Come with us and use it for the good of all."

Léofric was amazed that they should know of his strange dreams. However, he was still reluctant to trust these strangers. "Bandits keep honeyed tongues between their teeth. How do I know for certain that you are not lying to me?"

The elf drew his scimitar. "I give you my word by the sacred tree of Varmiron, the first tree ever planted when the world was young, that you may trust us. Now, the Army has great need of you for reasons that must, for now, remain secret. You must trust us. Will you come?"

Léofric had heard that the words of elves were bound with honor and he believed in their wisdom, so, despite his original distrust, he began to believe that what they said was true.

His mind flew through the fond childhood memories of the years he had spent with his mother. He was silent for a time. Was he truly able to leave her? No. And yet, here was the chance for which he had been waiting. He felt a tugging at his heart, as if his unknown destiny were beckoning him. Finally, Léofric found words. "I shall come. I beg you; let me go bid my mother goodbye."

The red warrior sighed, "Alas, that you cannot do. Our time is precious. Your duty with us must remain a secret and not even your mother may know where you have gone. She would only try to hinder your leaving. Sometimes you must simply start down a road without looking back."

A shadow passed over Léofric's face for a moment. He would be leaving the only life he had ever known. But could this be the only chance he would ever have to discover who his father was? His mind flew fleetingly home to his mother, and then he was resolved to go. Léofric nodded his agreement.

The red-haired man smiled and then turned to the chestnut stallion. He took a hauberk and light broadsword from the satchel. "You won't need them here, but you had best wear this armor and train with this sword for when the time comes. Can you ride?"

Léofric nodded, not wanting these seasoned warriors to know that the only beast he had ever ridden was a farm mule, which was very different from riding a warhorse.

Wulf indicated the chestnut stallion. "This is Haldor, and you may ride him. It will take time getting used to the mail, but you will have to."

Wulf helped Léofric pull the hauberk over his head. Léofric felt weighted down by the many steel rings, and at first, it was extremely hard to move, especially for a farm boy who had worn light, loose-fitting garments for all of his life. But, following Wulf's example, Léofric was soon able to move more comfortably.

The two warriors felled some branches with their swords for firewood, as that was scarce on the plain. They shoved this firewood into their already bulging saddlebags. As the noonday sun scattered on the forest floor, the three travelers made their way north past the trees, and as the setting sun gleamed on their mail, they reached the open plain. Léofric did not know what awaited him, but something in his heart had told him to go with these strangers. It was a chance he was willing to take, no matter the cost.

THREE
THE WOLVES OF FIRBOLG FOREST

The plain of central Irminsul was a wide expanse of tall, billowing golden grass, seeming to rise heavenward to meet the crystal blue sky. Occasionally, rabbits and squirrels could be seen running among the tall golden blades, and solitary stalks of wheat grew here and there. The sun shone down brightly during the day, but it was spring and not overly warm. The nights were cool and refreshing, the stars shining down brightly through the dark blue sky. On several occasions, the nocturnal grasshoppers could be seen, seeming to dance rhythmically before the moon as they sprang among the golden stalks.

They rode their horses for weeks through the tall waving grass, stopping for only a few precious moments around midday for a meager meal. They slept under the stars and would recommence their journey shortly after sunrise and a quick breakfast. For the first few days, the three companions ate from the men's store of dried venison and mutton. Léofric was comforted by the thought that he had brought his bow with him and could use it to renew their meat supply once it began to dwindle.

As they cantered along day by day at a quick pace, Léofric wondered about all that Wulf had said at their first meeting in the forest. He had decided to follow the blue-eyed man so hastily that he had not found an opportunity to ask him either about his strange "gift" or his father. What could this gift be? And why should the Army need it? The warrior seemed loath to speak of either subject and quickened the pace with each passing day. But as they reached the center of the plain, Wulf slowed somewhat. Still, Léofric did not find the courage for the questions that he longed to ask the mighty soldier.

The dark elf passed the time by singing long, beautiful songs in Elvish. Léofric could never understand the words, but the beautiful, flowing, rhythmic sounds stirred his heart in a way he could not quite describe. He longed to ask Surgessar what the words meant, but never found the opportunity, as there was never an opening for conversation of that kind, the men talking mostly of the need for haste. Ever since he was young, Léofric had heard of and longed to learn the beautiful speech of the elves, even though the superstitious people of the Southlands disparaged it as arcane and wicked.

One day, during the midday meal, Wulf said, "Léofric, the time has come for you to learn to defend yourself, as you never had the opportunity to use a sword living in the Southlands. Come. Let us move away from the fire." He rose and walked a short distance from the fire.

Then began a vigorous session of training in the art of the blade. "Attack me," the red-haired man commanded.

Léofric swung at him clumsily in a diagonal motion, first from the left, then from the right, and each time Wulf dodged the blow easily. As the boy swung through again, Wulf planted a quick foot on the boy's chest as his blade neared the ground and knocked him flat on his back. Looking down sternly at him, Wulf chided, "Never overextend your stroke. There, you are vulnerable and off balance."

Helping the flustered boy to his feet, Wulf said, "The primary power of a thrust comes from the shoulders and arms working in unison. Make sure to hold the hilt firmly, but not so tightly that your adversary has the chance to knock it from your grasp with a quick parry. I know you are strong enough for powerful thrusts. Here, let me show you the proper technique."

Wulf thrust his massive blade forward in a swift, concentrated motion, his corded muscles rippling as they straightened. "There. Now you try."

Léofric took a deep breath, doing his best to concentrate solely on the motion of his arms, and then painstakingly thrust his blade forward, falling flat on his face in the process. The blade of his sword ran lightly through the front of his boot, affecting a large gash and nearly cutting off his toe.

Chuckling softly to himself, the broad-shouldered warrior picked the boy up and set him on his feet. "I advise you to practice that as often as possible. Do not worry. We will find you some new boots at the camp."

Wulf showed him various other attacks and parries, and was very insistent that the boy learn them and practice them perfectly.

"No! No!" thundered the red giant. "You must thrust with your elbows completely straight! Parry to the left and not the right. Put all the muscles in your back into your stroke, like so."

This went on for several days, until finally Wulf allowed Léofric to spar with him. At the first stroke, the red-haired warrior parried violently, then hooked his booted foot behind Léofric's and knocked the young man flat on his back.

"You need to work more on your footwork. Always expect the least-expected movement on the part of your adversary."

On another occasion, Léofric moved to thrust at Wulf, but the red-haired soldier stepped aside as Léofric flew past, tripping the boy over his mailed knee. Léofric fell flat on his face, his mouth filled with foul-tasting grass. The red-bearded man burst into fits of laughter.

"Give me your hand," Wulf said, reaching down to help the boy up. Thinking quickly, Léofric pulled down hard with one hand and with the other, brought up his sword to Wulf's neck. A look of surprise crossed the red-haired man's face.

"Remind me," the boy said, smiling. "What was so amusing?"

A huge grin spread across the soldier's lips. "You have the quick wit of your mother, to be sure, boy."

Léofric wondered for a moment at this statement, as he did not know how this soldier from the north could know anything of his mother, but then lightly dismissed it.

There were many other such instances as these. Wulf always had the upper hand. Slowly, however, Léofric began to hold his own in the bouts. Once, when the training had been particularly hard, they locked blades and, for a time, Léofric was pushed almost to the ground. Summoning every ounce of strength that remained in his overtaxed muscles, with a great grunt he pushed his adversary to the ground.

"Never overexert your muscles, Wulf," Léofric said half-mockingly, a smart grin on his face. "If you do, you are vulnerable and off balance." The red man grinned slightly at the irony of hearing his own words come from the lips of another.

"Well," he said, coming up looking very pleased and astonished, "I see that you have learned something. That is good. You will need these skills when the time comes."

One morning, Léofric awoke to find that there had been a light spring rain during the night. He did not see the dark elf or the red-haired man, and assumed they were out scouting ahead. He decided to put himself to use and start the breakfast fire. He walked over to the satchel that contained the firewood, his shirt billowing slightly in the cool morning breeze. Léofric reached in and pulled out several logs, gasping as he touched them. Light though it had been, the night rain had soaked what remained of their supply of logs, rendering them useless. Léofric gingerly touched the soaked bark and sighed in despair.

"What shall we do now?" he asked, bewildered.

"Leave that to me," answered a familiar deep voice with a knowledgeable air. Léofric whirled to see that Surgessar and Wulf had returned while he was preoccupied with the wood.

Clearing a space, the dark-skinned elf gathered up some stalks of grass and laid them in front of him. Leaning forward, he shouted, "Aelgaelis!"

There was a flash of light and the stalks crackled into the flame.

Léofric stared at the fire disbelievingly. "What was that? How did you do that?"

Surgessar smiled. "It is the ancient language of my people. When spoken with extreme concentration it can perform magic, or, more correctly, what most humans perceive to be 'magic'. This is not the evil magic of the Dark Enemy. No. Rather, it is the sacred power that the One who leads the everlasting fight against the Dark Enemy has entrusted to my people. I will tell you more of Him later. Now, the word I just said a moment ago is the Elvish word for 'fire'. You will need to learn Elvish to be able to better use your gift."

Léofric was greatly pleased at the prospect of learning the beautiful Elvish language. Here also was an opportunity to uncover the mystery of what Wulf and the dark elf had said concerning him, so he asked, "What is my gift?"

"The phenomenon of your dreams of battle is called 'sword dreaming'. You are the Sword Dreamer. Through your dreams and concentration, you are able to see the mind of your enemy."

"But how can this be?"

"It is not yet time for you to know the secret source of sword dreaming. When the time is right you will be told."

Surgessar left Wulf to tend to breakfast and led Léofric several yards away from the fire.

"In most instances, sword dreaming happens at night when you are asleep," the elf said in his deep resonant voice. "That is the clearer sword dream. This is what you had been experiencing in the barn on your farm. Many times, however, the Sword Dreamer needs to tap into his enemy's mind when it is day. This requires much deeper concentration than does sword dreaming at night, while you sleep."

He made Léofric stand with his back to him. "Close your eyes, concentrate. Try your hardest to tap into my mind."

Léofric closed his eyes and breathed deeply. At first he only felt the wind on his face and heard his own breathing. Then the colors swam in front of his eyes and he felt his mind leaving his body. Then, as if through a mist-shrouded veil, he saw himself standing facing the other direction. He felt the rhythmic breathing of the elf as if it was his own. He felt the elf's powerful legs running forward, but they made no sound. He saw his image becoming larger and larger as the elf approached. He caught the glint of steel in the morning sun and in a second his image filled the whole vision. He quickly swept his sword up in a quick parry and, detachedly, he felt the force of the blow descend on his lifted blade.

His mind reunited with his body. Then he opened his eyes and heard a rolling sound like a clap of thunder. He realized that it was Surgessar, and he was laughing. Léofric turned to see the elf doubled over with the merriment of his success.

"Well done. Well done, Sword Dreamer. You are learning fast. We will continue our training as we progress on our journey. You must hone your skills. But now I see that breakfast is ready. Come. Let us go eat."

One night, about a week later, as Surgessar prepared the evening meal over a crackling fire, Léofric leaned in close and asked, "Surgessar, are you well-versed in the Elven lore?"

The dark elf looked up at the diamond-studded sky, and the red-gold light of the fire danced on his ebon skin as he answered. "As well-versed as any of my people. Why do you ask?"

"Your people are the oldest race in the world. I want to know everything, back to the beginning."

"Mercy," cried Surgessar, suddenly overwhelmed. "Were I to tell you of all the kingdoms of my race of old, and the Song of the Seven Stars that Gildéador Himself composed, and all the kingdoms that He holds in His hand, I should be talking here till the end of my days, long though they are."

"Who is Gildéador?"

"He is The King That Is. From Him comes all that is and ever will be. Long ago, He was known of men, though few of them know or speak His name now in these dark days. He is known in another place by a different Name, a Name too holy for even elves to speak. Someday I will teach you more of the lore of my people."

Despite his first impressions of the man, Léofric found himself growing fonder and fonder of Wulf. It was strange but, in a way, Léofric felt something closer than friendship, almost a bond of forgotten kinship, with the mighty soldier.

Often the red-haired giant would sit at the campfire, laugh loudly and tell Léofric tales of the many battles that he and Surgessar had fought together. Strangely, the soldier did not reveal very much about himself and never spoke of his family, if he had any at all.

One night, as the embers were dying and after Surgessar had gone to sleep, Léofric plucked up his courage and asked, "Wulf, do you have a family?"

Wulf looked away and his throat tightened somewhat. Finally, he said, "I did once. I do not know if I will find them again."

"My mother says that if you keep persevering, you will obtain your heart's desires if they are pure. Finding one's family is surely a pure desire."

"Well, maybe after the war is won, I shall find them again." The red-haired man sighed and turned away.

One morning soon after this incident, Wulf discovered that their meat supply was running dangerously low. The three travelers were unperturbed by this however, as Léofric's skill with the bow was put to good use.

"You are a good shot, my boy," Wulf told him jovially. "Though, truly, I cannot speak from experience, but I was almost able to." Léofric laughed. The soldier was referring to their first meeting.

Whenever Léofric brought back a kill, no matter the size, Wulf praised him loudly and with gusto, as if he was his own son.

Once, when he returned with a brace of coneys, Wulf exclaimed, "Well done. Well shot, my boy. When we reach the camp of Futhark, we shall give you a proper longbow and a quiver of steel-tipped arrows."

Then Léofric said cautiously, "Do not misunderstand me, Wulf. I am grateful for your praise. But it seems to me that you are too generous with it. I am not vexed by it in any way, but forgive me, for I cannot help my curiosity. I must ask: why do you praise me so?"

A look of pensive sadness lingered for a moment over the red-bearded giant's eyes. Then he said, "I have become very fond of you and you remind me of someone I once knew."

Léofric wanted to talk more on the subject, but he saw by Wulf's expression that the soldier was in no mood to speak further of the matter. So he merely kept his thoughts to himself and helped prepare the meal.

After several more days of quick traveling, they came to their first major decision and obstacle: the dark and foreboding Firbolg Forest. This was one of the largest forests in all of Irminsul, over eighteen leagues across. The trees were the tallest in the whole country.

They came upon it at midday. Tall, imposing oaks, rising like the bastions of an emerald fortress, formed the walls. The moss and ivy that completely covered the trees gave them an appearance of golem-like vitality and power; the massive branches and deep roots supporting a sturdy stock resembled the mighty creatures. Strange sounds came from the interior, like a mixture of the screeching of crows and the moaning of the noonday spring wind through the trees.

"It is said," remarked Wulf, looking stoically at the foreboding oaks, "that giant wolves live in this forest. Their favorite meal is human flesh. Best be on your guard. We must stay close together."

Suddenly, all the folktales that Léofric had heard in his childhood came flooding back to him, tales of the evil spirits dwelling in the hollows of trees, waiting to feast on the soul of an unlucky traveler. He held back as Wulf advanced to the moss-covered trees.

"I do not wish to go through there," Léofric said, his voice quavering a little. "Can we not go around it?"

"Doing so would mean several more days of traveling, and every hour is precious," said Wulf, dismounting. "It is only a three hour walk directly through. We must take our chances, wolves or no. The roots are too thick for riding. We must lead the horses through. The mission to bring you to the camp of the Army of King Futhark was entrusted to me, and I shall keep you safe."

Léofric sighed hopelessly, and, acquiescing, followed the giant soldier into the forest. He felt the old superstitions churn his stomach, but he had come to trust the red soldier almost as a father, so he did not try to turn back.

The sunlight scattered in patches through the green canopy. Mist rose from the ground, proving it impossible for the travelers to see more than a few feet in front of them. Surgessar's Elven eyes were keen and perceptive, so he took the lead.

Léofric noticed that even Wulf was being affected by the eerie, foreboding forest, as he kept one hand up on the hilt of his massive sword at all times. Though they saw no forest creatures or malevolent spirits, the superstitions of the Southlands were still fresh and vivid in Léofric's mind.

After they had walked for about two and a half hours, Surgessar halted suddenly. Holding up one ebon hand, he pressed the forefinger of the other to his lips.

Léofric's eyes darted around the clearing, quickly taking in the surroundings that might aid in a quick escape if need be. There was a moss-covered stump to the left near where Wulf was standing. Behind them was a fallen tree trunk perched diagonally on its broken trunk. To the right were a pile of fallen logs stacked by nature one on top of the other.

"What do you sense?" Wulf hissed, coming up behind him cautiously.

"Wolves. Several of them. They are very close. These wolves have a taste for man and elf flesh. They will not bother with the horses." The dark elf's hand moved to the silver wire-wrapped hilt of his broad-bladed scimitar.

Wulf laid a hand on Léofric's shoulder and whispered, "Climb that high stump several paces away; the one that looks as if a giant sawed the tree in half. There you will be safe. We can still reasonably communicate over such a short distance." Léofric quickly complied.

Turning silently on his heel, the elf looked intently up at the young man. "You must tap into their minds before they are on top of us. It will be very hard, but you must try. To help you concentrate during the day you must say the Elvish word for 'night': Aergerion."

Léofric closed his eyes tightly. Small beads of sweat, like tiny pearls, began to glisten on his brow. He could not concentrate. His mind was racing with thoughts of ravenous wolves and dancing malevolent forest spirits determined to end the travelers' existence. Then his mind locked into place. Taking a deep breath, he firmly said, "Aergerion."

Immediately his vision was doubly darkened. Slowly his mind left his body. He felt the hot breath of a wolf. He sensed its brutal animality. He felt its powerful fours pawing the damp fallen foliage as it came.

Suddenly, a mailed back and fiery mane became visible, behind it the moss-covered stump that he knew, from memory, was on his physical right. Without opening his eyes, Léofric shouted, "Wulf, behind you!"

The mighty man whirled, his broadsword slashed in a downward sweep, and a gigantic gray wolf carcass fell headless to the ground.

"Well done!" Wulf said, but Léofric did not hear.

In his mind, he felt a gigantic body leaping over fallen tree trunks. Those were undoubtedly the trunks to the right of the clearing. In a moment, he saw a mailed shoulder covered by a blue surcoat, growing larger and larger.

"To the right, Surgessar!"

The warning came not a moment too soon. The dark elf swung his curved blade so powerfully that the beast was completely brained. Surgessar's eyes twinkled, and for a fleeting second, the elf congratulated himself for being an effective teacher.

Léofric could tell from the growling in his head that several of the small pack still lived, and he informed his companions of this while still in meditation.

He saw, apparently from one wolf crawling low to the ground, a pair of brown deerskin boots. He could not tell whose they were, as both the elf and the man wore the same style of boots. He was about to speak but held his breath.

In the blinking of an eye, Wulf felt himself being knocked on his back by a massive body. Thinking quickly, he held out his sword in front of him and as his mailed back hit the forest floor, the attacking wolf was spit upon the blade. Straining his massive muscles, the red soldier forced the hulking carcass off his body and wrenched his great sword free.

Before Léofric had a chance to see the next plan of attack, Wulf was again knocked on his back by yet another muscular gray beast. His broadsword was knocked out of his hands and he rolled with the snarling mass of fur and teeth across the forest floor. Léofric saw this in his mind, but knew that if he spoke or cried out, the distraction would prove fatal.

Thinking quickly, Wulf thrust his shoulders forward and rolled back until the blade was just out of reach. Keeping his head and hands out of the reach of the snapping jaws, he fumbled and fingered for his sword. At last grasping the leather-covered hilt, he pulled back his mailed arms and drove the blade as deep as he could into the beast's mouth. Its whimper turned into a gurgle and fresh blood stained the blade.

By this time, Léofric had refocused his mind. He was looking from a high vantage point down onto the forest floor on the south side of the clearing, and he saw a tall, dark-haired figure standing facing the opposite direction. The vision was closing in on the figure at a terrifying pace.

He suddenly realized what was happening and cried, "Behind you, elf!"

Surgessar whirled with his crossbow and fired, striking the beast in midair, and not a moment too soon, for the beast fell, a bolt through its throat, but three inches from the elf.

"Is that the last?" Wulf asked, panting and sweating like a strained horse.

Léofric concentrated for a moment. He felt and saw nothing. "That is the last of them."

For a moment they stood there, panting from their exertions. Léofric was the most exhausted of all. Surgessar noticed this.

"Sword dreaming during the day is very exhausting," the dark elf said as Léofric climbed down and rejoined them. "But we are almost out of the forest. When we reach the camp of the King, you can rest."

He bent to pick up the fallen wolf. Hoisting it over his shoulder, he said, "I shall make a cloak of the skin for you. This is a memento of your first victory. But remember, tapping into the mind of a beast and tapping into the mind of a man are two very different things. You may need the skills to do both."

Within a half hour, they reached the edge of the forest and saw the fluttering silver banners of the King on the horizon.

FOUR

ABANDONED

By the time Ragna awoke from her long tear-exhausted sleep, she looked up to notice that the golden rays of dusk were shooting through the window. She had dreamed of her long lost husband while sleeping at the table, wearied and saddened over her angry conversation with her son. The thought of evening suddenly yanked her mind back to the present. Léofric. He had not returned to the table and it was almost suppertime. With his growing appetite, the young man was never late for a meal.

She called for him. He did not answer. She looked for him in his room. He was not there. Then, she began to worry in earnest. It was not his habit to stay away for long, even on the rare occasion that he was angry. What could have happened to him? He could have been waylaid by a stray wolf or a country thug. She grimaced, for she knew he was less than popular in the surrounding area because of his quiet behavior. She disliked the men of the village, but she had never thought them capable of such things. Oh, if only she had not let her emotions run away from her. Her beloved son could be lying wounded because of her unruly temper.

She rose quickly and hurried out the door. Coming outside, she looked frantically first to the right and then to the left, desperately searching for a sign of her missing son. She noticed the heavy imprints of his booted feet in the green grass, trudging steadily in the direction of the woods that separated their home from the nearest village. It all became terribly clear to her in that moment. It struck her like a crossbow bolt through the heart. Léofric was not dead. He must have abandoned her to go seek his own. She put her golden head in her hands and sank down on her knees. The tears flowed freely.

"No," she thought in despair, "not again!" Her mind flew back to another terrible night when she had awoken at midnight to find herself alone and abandoned in the house.

After the sun had nearly disappeared over the western sky, she got up and walked slowly back to the house. Going into her room, she removed the feather-stuffed mattress from the bed frame. She picked up a brown leather purse which still held a few solitary gold coins, the last that remained of her dowry. A dowry for a man who had swept her off her feet, his eyes as sea-blue as Léofric's. She hoped it would be enough for her to survive until Léofric returned, if he ever returned. She felt as though she had been abandoned again, and it was a blow too heavy for her to bear.

She recalled the month she had spent as the young, beautiful bride of a strong country youth with whom she had been sweethearts for years. She realized later that she had been walking in a world of fanciful dreams, on a thin cloud that kept her for a time separated from reality. When her handsome husband had abandoned her, her world of silver glass had come crashing down. Luckily a kind old woman of the village had taken her in and cared for her. The other villagers had looked down on her for being so blissfully naïve when she had married, and snickered behind their hands as she passed. It was one of the many pains she learned to bear during the several grief-stricken years she lived with the kind old woman.

At first she talked often of her lost husband, longing for him to return. But one night, on the anniversary of her wedding day, her bitterness and resentment boiled over, and she resolved to never again speak of him, not even to her child, though deep in her heart she longed to feel the security the strong embrace had given her.

When the baby was old enough, and she had regained her dignity, strength, and will to survive, she had thanked and bid good-bye to the old widow and bought the farm she and her husband had lived in for a month with a large portion of her dowry, for her husband had not taken any of it when he had abandoned her that night several years before. She then hid the rest to keep it for her son when he came of age, for she wanted him to have some security, security that she had not been fortunate enough to have when she was a youth. Even so, she disliked the idea of him ever marrying, as she did not want him to experience the pain and betrayal that she had experienced when she had fallen in love. In her heart, she truly believed that all marriages ended in betrayal and heartache. And yet, she could not help longing for the love that she had lost. So every night without fail, she secretly wept for her lost husband.

She had been unaccustomed to farm work, being the daughter of a village weaver, but her husband was gone and her father had disowned her for the shame of what had happened to her, so it was labor she was forced to learn. For several years she arose early in the morning, before baby Léofric awoke, and tended to the farm, becoming very strong and fit in the process. Then she would tend to her son for the rest of the day. It truly was a joy as well as a relief to her when Léofric grew old enough to take over the more physically taxing duties. She had vowed to herself that her son would not follow in the footsteps of his father. That was why she was most distressed when he began showing interest in becoming a warrior as he grew older, for his father had been a warrior before returning to marry her.

But now all the painful, heart-wrenching memories came flooding back. Léofric must have abandoned her. Surely he had followed the path of his uncaring father, though he knew not who his father was. It was in his blood to abandon those he had professed to love, in the blood of his father, which ran pure in his veins. She laid her head in her hands and wept anew.

FIVE

MANY MEETINGS

Another hour's ride brought the three travelers to the camp of the Army of Irminsul. The camp seemed almost a town unto itself, a vast array of tents of silver cloth buzzing with activity. Countless mail-clad men in steel caps and open-faced helms called barbutes moved among the tents on different errands. Scattered among the many silver bivouacs were tuns of ale, around which the tall mail-clad soldiers talked, smoked pipes and laughed. In the center of the camp was set the large pavilion of the King. The banner of Irminsul, a white unicorn on a field of silver, flapped in the breeze before it.

Set a safe distance away from the tents were small smithies where sweaty armorers in dirty aprons stoked the fires and repaired nicks and cuts in mail and weapons. Sheep, cows, and other livestock lowed, bleated and squealed in makeshift pins. These had been sent as a food supply for the Army from Auraheim. Strong stallions meant for cavalry charges were tethered to stakes outside the tents, where they neighed, huffed and absent-mindedly pawed the earth. Before the outbreak of the war, the cavalry force of the Army of Irminsul had numbered well over one hundred thousand men and horses. It still consisted of several score thousand mail-clad riders and armored horse, for the primary strength of the rebels was infantry. In this regard, they greatly outnumbered the forces of the King.

The silver tents sparkled brightly in the afternoon sun, giving the camp an aura of majesty. The only blemishes on the scene were the horrendous odors wafting from the horses and livestock.

The three travelers rode up and were greeted by a dark-bearded man in mail bearing a hand axe with an extended shaft on his shoulder. His sparkling green eyes plainly showed his merry demeanor. Strangely, the man saluted as Wulf rode up. Wulf returned the greeting.

"Hail, Halifar." the red giant exclaimed, smiling.

"Hail, general."

Wulf fell silent, and Léofric froze in disbelief.

"You told me you were a soldier," Léofric cried, feeling both a sense of incredible awe coupled with slight anger at the deception. "You did not say you were a general."

"Calm down, Léofric!" Wulf remonstrated. "I knew you would not come with me if you knew I was a general, for you would not believe a general would take such an interest in you. I had to keep my position in the Army a secret from you."

"But…"

Léofric's protest was cut short by Surgessar crying something aloud in Elvish. He leaped off his horse, and ran to embrace a tall figure who came to meet him. Léofric heard a soothing female voice speaking in Elvish.

"Elsté, addag. Rhinonín anathi?"

Surgessar returned with his arm around an elf girl who appeared to be about Léofric's age. Léofric caught his breath sharply and did his best not to stare in dumbstruck awe. The Elven girl was the exact girl he had seen in his dreams. She was tall and dark of skin with beautiful brown eyes that seemed to pierce the young man's soul. Her long midnight black hair fell well past her shoulders. She was apparently a fighter, for she was dressed in a brigandine of purple cloth. The mail sewn on the cloth jerkin brightly reflected the late afternoon sunlight. She bore two sickle-bladed swords in a double baldric on her back.

Surgessar said proudly, "Léofric, this is my daughter, Súndéa. She shall teach you Elvish to increase your power as the Sword Dreamer."

The beautiful elf bowed politely in greeting and said, "Welcome to the camp of the Army of Irminsul. It shall be both an honor and a privilege to assist the Sword Dreamer."

"And-and-I-I shall be most grateful," said Léofric, turning slightly red in the face.

The elf's laugh was like the tinkling of a silver bell. She looked worriedly at the torn boot he wore. "Give those to me for the night. I shall see what I can do with them." Léofric smiled sheepishly and handed them to her, not knowing what to think. The tall grass was soft and did not bother his exposed feet.

At that moment, Halifar returned and, saluting, said, "I am sorry, General, but I must inform you that the King is seriously ill. In fact, the leech has said that he may have only a few days of life left. Forgive me for not speaking of this earlier. I was too overjoyed to see that you had come safely through the Firbolg. He has asked that only his captains meet with him. Not even the Sword Dreamer is to come. He does not wish to see the Sword Dreamer until everything is set in order. He has asked specifically for you, General." Upon hearing this, Wulf quickly took his leave.

For the rest of the evening, Léofric wandered among the silver tents of the camp, making the acquaintance of soldier and page alike. Long did he linger by the forges of the weapon smiths. Never before had he seen so many swords, axes, maces, helms, and mail coats, though in truth, he had never seen any weapons or armor of any consequence before in his life. The closest thing on his farm to a weapon had been the axe he had used for chopping wood.

Upon a great table lined with newly-forge gleaming swords, he found a magnificent sword apparently of Elvish make. What it was doing in the camp of the Army of Irminsul, Léofric could not surmise, unless it belonged to Surgessar. Its blade was of a deep blue steel, inscribed with Elvish runes, and reflected the late evening light as the sea reflects the noonday sun on a clear day.

The boy was amazed at its lightness as he picked it up. Its blade was broad and shaped somewhat like a willow leaf, widening out from the hilt and then tapering to an almost rounded point.

He was still admiring its master craftsmanship when he heard a commanding voice say, "Put that down!"

Léofric turned to see a short bald man in a smith's leather apron running to where Léofric stood. His eyes betrayed frustration and worry, so Léofric complied with his short command.

The man stopped and breathed a sigh of relief. He stood only about five feet tall, and he wore a short, bushy black beard splotched with gray. Although he was short, the muscles of his arms and chest bulged, apparently having been strengthened by years of working at the forge.

The strong man smiled. "I am sorry to have startled you, boy. I am Kettil, chief smith of the camp, and that sword is my most prized possession. It was made by one of the master smiths of Aelgaelisel far in the northern territory of the Evenlands, and I procured it at great expense. Surgessar tells me that Aelgaelisel mean 'land of fire' in the Elvish tongue. That land produces the best weapons and armor in the Elvenlands. It is partly because of the priceless ore, Firgram iron, that is only found there, and also because of the mountains of fire that dot the landscape. Do you know how the master smiths of Aelgaelisel produce their priceless weapons and armor? No? Then I shall tell you. They journey up to the crags of the mountains, where the fire flows, and brave the heat for days, beating out their creations on the anvil. It is for this reason the elves of Aelgaelisel are called 'fire elves'. The fire is so hot that the steel keeps its blue color even after it has cooled. Say, you are the Sword Dreamer, are you not? You come from the Southlands, do you? So do I, originally. Well, if you ever need a good weapon, old Kettil will always be at your service."

Léofric smiled. He liked the jovial, loquacious old smith.

Léofric saw very little of Wulf the next few days. The red general spent most of his time in the pavilion of the King. Léofric himself was preoccupied with the Elvish lessons taught by Súndéa.

Surgessar brought him to the first lesson the day after they arrived in camp. As he approached, Léofric saw the dark elf girl holding his boots, and the one that was torn had been made whole.

She handed them to Léofric and said, "Please, look inside."

Léofric peeked inside the boots and saw to his astonishment that they had been lined with rich, soft, cream-colored fur.

Surgessar looked at his daughter disapprovingly. "That fur is undoubtedly from your best winter cloak. Why did you do this?"

Súndéa smiled and shrugged. "It is no longer winter, addag. I thought it a fitting gift for the Sword Dreamer."

The ebon-skinned warrior grunted and turned to leave. Léofric stared at Súndéa. No one had ever given him so rich a gift.

Léofric many times tried to overcome his fear and tell Súndéa of how she had appeared in his dreams, but that he could never do. It appeared to Léofric that she regarded him merely as an amusing country bumpkin, though she would compliment him often on his progress in learning Elvish, so he could never tell what she truly thought of him. Her behavior around him seemed inconsistent.

The lessons continued on and on until Léofric knew a wide smattering of words and grammar. At times she would tell him specific words which pertained to sword dreaming, and at times he would ask her out of curiosity and she was always ready to indulge him.

"What is the Elvish word for 'wind'?"

"That is Galathon."

"And 'star'?"

"Cluadrim."

"And for 'stream'?"

"Galanead."

One evening, as the setting sun painted the sky in pink and orange gold, Léofric sat with Súndéa, having an Elvish lesson. They had already learned ten words that evening, as well as the proper conjugations of some difficult verbs, and the lesson was coming to a close. Léofric plucked up his courage and decided to put a plan that he had been forming in his head into action.

"Súndéa," he said cautiously, "what is the Elvish word for 'love'?"

The elf girl smiled. "That is Léofric."

Léofric stared in disbelief. "That is a lie!"

"Yes. But it is a good lie." She put her arms around his neck and pressed her lips to his.

As the days turned into weeks, Léofric began spending more time with Halifar. He found the man to be one of the most jovial in all of the camp. Léofric would often take his supper with him and, as they ate, the young captain would sing songs of ancient battles and romances. In fact, Léofric learned more of the folk literature of Irminsul from Halifar than he would have in any of the schools in the cities of the north.

One evening, as the sun was setting in the West, Léofric and Halifar were eating bowls of lamb stew and chatting.

"I tell you the truth, boy," the young captain said as he spooned another steaming bite into his mouth, "this is very tasty, but nothing compares to my wife's lamb stew. It is food fit for Futhark's banquet hall, the finest stew in all of Irminsul. When the war is over, you must come to my house in Auraheim for supper."

"Tell me, captain," Léofric said, "how do you know the general?"

Halifar smiled, reminiscing. "I was but a page when he became a general. The other pages were not kind to me. He noticed this and pitied me, so he took me under his wing and taught me to fight and how to be a soldier, and to live with honor. When the chance for elevation to captaincy came, he vouched for me before the King. A captain of pikemen by the name of Jarkin, who had been an older page and one of my principle taunters, was also vying for the position and hated me all the more when I was chosen to receive it."

"What became of that man?" Léofric asked.

"I know not, for he disappeared when the rebellion started. At any rate, I owe my success to the general. I have always thought of him as an older brother. You should be honored to know him and call him your friend."

"What will you do after the war is won?"

"I shall return to Auraheim and use my pension to open an inn, like my father kept when I was a lad. For me, there is no joy in fighting. However, I find comfort in the fact that I am fighting for my King and my country and those whom I hold dear. After the war, if I can live in peace, I will. Still, if need be, I would be proud to see my son bear my axe into battle after me."

Léofric had several other such conversations with Halifar over the next few days. He had never had a brother and felt a bond of almost fraternal kinship growing between him and the young, cheerful captain. A spirit of joy radiated out from Halifar to all who were around him, especially when he sang of the mighty deeds of warriors of old, as he loved to do. This supernatural joy spilled over into Léofric's heart and gave him a heart-warming energy that was so great it was almost indescribable.

One evening before supper a few days later, Léofric was sitting away from the camp, talking with Súndéa after finishing a lesson in Elvish, when Wulf came from the tent of the King.

"King Futhark is on death's doorstep. He has asked for you. Come."

Disappointed at having his time with Súndéa suddenly brought to an end, Léofric reluctantly followed Wulf to the tent of the King. Many soldiers and servants were before the great pavilion. Ducking inside, Léofric saw a tall, grey-bearded man clad in a robe of silver and black silk, lying on a royal bed, surrounded by his officers. His limbs had once been strong and agile, but now were withered by old age and sickness. The silver-coated hauberk and silver-hilted sword of the King lay hard by. The white unicorn standard on the field of silver hung above the head of the bed. A white quill and some parchment lay on a small table by the side of the bed. The round silver diadem of the king lay on a dais at the foot of the lacquered bed. Tapestries recording the names of Futhark's ancestors decorated the walls of the tent. All this contributed to the aura of majesty and authority.

As they entered, the old man's gray eyes followed the parting of the flap. He beckoned weakly for Wulf and Léofric to come near the bed. His eyes lingered on the young man.

"General Rothgaric?" he asked.

Léofric felt a wave of fresh anger come over him, despite the presence of the King and all the honor and glorious riches of his House that were evidenced by the fine decorations of the royal tent. The red-haired man had also lied about his name! Léofric had been deceived on another account, and that was all that concerned him at the moment. He did not care about the King, his troubles, or the war.

"This is the Sword Dreamer?" rasped Futhark, indicating Léofric.

"Yes, my King," replied the newly revealed Rothgaric.

Speaking to Léofric, the King said "It is unfortunate that I will not see the peace of my realm restored by your aid, as has been the duty of the Sword Dreamer since the days of Nilmeron, the El- ven ruler of Irminsul. The Sword Dreamer has protected this realm for all the days of my House, and so shall he do again."

To Rothgaric, he said, "I have no son to rule after me. I therefore place my kingdom in your capable hands. Do you, Roth- garic, swear to serve your people and champion the Silver City in all that you do, and also to love your people as a father?"

"I do, my King."

A look of peace came over the King's face. "My troubled days are over. I go now to dwell with my forebears, for peace shall be restored to Irminsul and the line of the Sword Dreamers shall continue, as it has since the days of Nilmeron." With that, the King closed his eyes and drifted off to sleep, but soon his chest ceased to rise and fall and he lay perfectly still.

For a time all was silent. Then Rothgaric said, "Prepare a fu- neral for your King." The captains left, leaving Rothgaric and Léof- ric alone in the tent.

"Why the deception?" Léofric demanded angrily, not giv- ing the slightest thought to the man's new authority. He lived in the Southlands, where the people did not care about the King or what he did. "Why did you bring me into this with honey sweet lies, away from my life and my mother, whom I love?"

"Partly, to save Irminsul. More importantly, because you are my son."

Léofric shook his head in disbelief. Rothgaric continued, "Look at your hair, a mixture of your mother's and mine. Your eyes are as sea-blue as mine. You are my son, and I love you."

Uncontrollable rage washed over Léofric. "No. How could you do this to your wife and son? For eighteen years I do not know who my father is, or even if he is alive. My mother is tortured every night by her grief. No. How could you? How-?" He turned and ran out of the tent.

For a time he sat away from the camp, his mind a burning and confused mass of racing thoughts. How could his father do this to him? Rothgaric did not love him or his mother, the wife he had so carelessly abandoned. Léofric could never forgive his father for his heartless decision.

He relived in his mind the countless times when he had seen his acquaintances at work in the fields with their fathers. He saw the many times at the summer fair in the village when he would see husbands and wives perusing the many stalls with their little ones. How he had longed for experiences such as these as he grew. He had also desired to dance in the country jigs and reels many times, but was afraid of being ridiculed because of his father. Because of this he had never danced or celebrated before in all his eighteen years.

The young husbands would buy trinkets for their pretty wives, and he often caught his mother, out of the corner of his eye, gazing at the couple longingly as they talked and laughed happily together. His father had taken that all away from her. And for what? Nonsense that he called battle glory. Léofric was disgusted that he had ever wanted to be a soldier. It was all very selfish of his father, and nothing he could say could bring back all the lost years.

When Léofric's anger had cooled somewhat, he sensed someone standing behind him. He turned. It was his father.

"Son," Rothgaric said compassionately, "I know you are angry. I understand your feelings, but you must hear me out. I left your mother out of necessity.

"You see, for centuries, the most honored position in the King's Army has been that of the Sword Dreamer. He has always ensured the victory for the King of Irminsul. Whenever a Sword Dreamer is about to die, he will make a sacred journey to the region of the Kjartens north of Auraheim. Somewhere, hidden among the peaks, is the forest of Bjor.

"Deep in the heart of that forest, flows the Geltenbach, the golden stream whose water is magical. The Sword Dreamer is guided on his journey by The King That Is. The Sword Dreamer will take water from the Geltenbach and give it to the King's most trusted general. The general will drink it, soon after he will marry, and his son will be the next Sword Dreamer.

"When I was a lad of fifteen, I lived in the Southlands, where I had been raised. I was courting your mother, and we planned to marry after a few years. But then the recruiters from Auraheim came to our village, and I was caught up in dreams of battle glory.

"I left your mother behind, joined the ranks, and fought with the Army for seven years, quickly rising from footman to captain, and finally becoming the youngest general in the entire army. Futhark soon noticed my skill, and I became his most trusted subordinate.

"Unbeknownst to the King, one of the highest generals in the Army, a black-hearted, conniving man named Gollmorn, was plotting to overthrow the King. But he knew he could not start a successful rebellion with the Sword Dreamer in his way. So he murdered the Sword Dreamer, Helgi, in his sleep before the poor old, feeble man had a chance to fight back.

"Gollmorn had already been stirring up insurrection and, gathering a large portion of the Army to himself, rose in rebellion.

Without the Sword Dreamer, we suffered defeat after defeat. Our forces began to dwindle, and a state of emergency was declared.

"I was sent by the King on a desperate mission, north into the northern Kjartens, to find the forest of Bjor and the Geltenbach. After months of searching, I found it. I took the water and drank it, hoping I would be forgiven the breach of tradition.

"Then I remembered your mother. I returned to the Southlands and sought her out. News of the northern wars seldom reaches the Southlands, as you know, so she did not know my true purpose in coming and I kept it from her, knowing that she would not understand. In fact, the day before I found you in the forest was our anniversary."

Léofric started. That was why his mother had been weeping so piteously the night before he left.

"A short while after the wedding, I received a message from the King saying that I was sorely needed back at the front lines. So I left without bidding your mother goodbye, for I knew she would not understand, especially as she was then carrying you inside. For over eighteen years we fought, knowing that the Sword Dreamer would be useless to us until he reached manhood.

"You must not be angry with me, son, for I did what I had to do. Often on the lonely nights before a hopeless battle, not knowing whether I would live or die, I thought of you and your mother and if I would ever see her again or ever have the chance to know you.

"When Gollmorn is defeated, I shall send for and renew my vows to your mother, as is proper after all these years. So you must be the Sword Dreamer, not only to save your country, but also to save your family. Please my son, forgive me."

At that moment, Léofric's ill will broke, for he finally understood and respected the deep sense of duty that propelled Rothgaric to action. He flew into the arms of his father.

Léofric, caught in a loving embrace, let his tears flow without holding them back. He had finally found what he needed: a strong dependable yet gentle hand to help guide him to his purpose. He had a wise, more experienced, yet kindred spirit, and knowing this provided him with a peace and assurance that his mother could never give.

When at last his tears had dried, Léofric knelt and proffered his sword. As the last pinkish light of the sun faded into the west, he said solemnly, "I, Léofric, Sword Dreamer, vow to serve you and love you as my father and as my King."

Rothgaric raised his son to his feet and together they returned to camp. Léofric had found his father at last. What is more, The King That Is had given him a purpose through his father, a place where he belonged.

SIX

PIKES ON THE RIDGE

The next morning at dawn, the body of Futhark was prepared for burial. During this time, it lay on a great oaken table carved with scenes of victories in battles from the days when Helgi was the Sword Dreamer. The King's body was anointed in the tent by the surgeons of the Army with many sweet-smelling perfumes such as jasmine and myrrh. These had been prepared especially for him by the healers of Auraheim, who had loved him as a father.

During his reign, Futhark had organized their sisterhood of healers and herbalists who cared for those of the city who could not afford a physician, though in truth their skill was greater than that of the best physicians of Auraheim. He had paid their expense out of his own personal store of gold, for which generosity he was loved by them and all the people of the city.

According to tradition, the silvered mail and sword of the King was passed down to his successor, so the body of Futhark was clad in plain mail, but it nevertheless reflected the light of the rising sun, which gave it the appearance of shining like the fading stars. Over this he wore a silver surcoat emblazoned with the white unicorn of Auraheim. A slender broadsword with a great pearl for a pommel, which he had used in his younger days as High Prince of Irminsul, lay clasped in his arms. After all the years of strife that had sat heavy upon his brow, in death, his face bore an expression of everlasting peace. His spirit had gone at last to the halls of his fathers.

Outside the royal tent, all the men in the Army, scores of thousands in number, from the highest captain to the lowest page had come to pay their respects to the departed King. Rothgaric, now proclaimed as the heir apparent, stood before the assembly and said, "Hail, Futhark, King of Irminsul." He brandished his sword. To those assembled before him, he said, "Know this, soldiers of Irminsul. I shall lead you but I shall not wear the armor or diadem of the king, nor shall I use his sword, until I feel I am worthy and am sure of victory."

A great rectangular sarcophagus of alabaster and silver had been wrought to house the body of the King. Upon this, Surgessar had carved with a dagger ancient Elvish runes which read, when translated into human speech: "Futhark, last King of the House of Nilmeron". It was to Futhark that Surgessar had sworn allegiance after fighting for years as a mercenary in the Army of Irminsul, as many elves of Nilmeronel had done in years past before the rebellion began.

The body was bourn to the sarcophagus on a litter formed with long spears. The litter was followed by a herald clad in a silver surcoat emblazoned with the white unicorn of Irminsul. His face was as grave as that of a carven statue.

The litter was carried by the personal bodyguards of the King, men in shining mail and gray surcoats matching that of the herald. With the greatest caution, they stoically lowered the body into the great coffin. Then it was solemnly sealed.

The herald then proclaimed in a resounding voice, "Hail, Futhark, King of Irminsul!"

The soldiers echoed the cry and brandished their swords. The rising sun flashed brilliantly on thousands of drawn blades. After a moment of standing frozen, as stone before a mausoleum, the men sheathed their swords. In that moment, they had stood as still as one of the marble statues that stood along many of the streets of Auraheim, of which Léofric had heard but had never seen. It was a glorious sight, one he would never forget.

First, Rothgaric approached the sarcophagus and inclined his head. Then the captains and all else assembled followed suit.

When Surgessar approached, he inclined his head and said softly, "Lasta, Gilda Irminsularion."

Léofric bowed in his turn, and then returned to stand by Surgessar. "It is highly sorrowful," the dark elf said. "Centuries ago, an Elvish prince, Nilmeron of Gladdéas, married a princess of Irminsul, Luaria the Fair. Since that union, the King has always had Elvish blood flowing in his veins. Now the line of the half-Elven Kings of Irminsul is ended."

The sarcophagus was buried beneath the grassy plain with a number of silver-tipped spears planted in the ground as a memorial. So passed Futhark, the last of the half-Elven Kings.

After the burial, preparations were made to meet the forces of Gollmorn. Scouts reported that a large body of rebel cavalry was camped in the rocky hill country to the east. Horses were saddled and bridled, tents were struck, and the Army marched westward toward the foothills of the western portion of the northern Kjartens.

The march would have seemed very monotonous to all were it not for the undying cheerfulness of Halifar. He rode with the personal counselors of the King, his raven mane blowing like a banner in the wind as he sang the time-honored ballads of Irminsul's warriors of old. His loud laughter rolled across the plain, and Léofric was glad of his company.

Rothgaric spoke very little, and would often ride quietly upon his stallion, keeping his eyes concentrated on the path ahead of him. He seemed very hesitant of his new authority, as if he was unsure whether or not he deserved it. He seemed reluctant to wield it, like a young country boy who had received his first knife and was afraid he would cut himself with it.

As they neared the western side of the northern Kjartens, the terrain became rougher and their pace slowed considerably. The road was marked with outcroppings of rocks, mountain brush and brambles. Yet still, within two fortnights' time, they saw on the horizon the black banners bearing the red falcon of the rebels.

It was as red as blood, the blood of the countless men of Irminsul that Gollmorn had slain. He was willing to slay countless more to achieve the mad dream that had long ago consumed his whole being. The same enmity that had burned in his heart for Futhark was now added to his already seething hatred of Rothgaric. These fused hatreds gave more fuel to the fire of his ambitions, and the sight of his enemy set his wicked mind scheming anew. He was desperate to find the perfect plan to bring about the downfall of his foes, and pave his road to kingship and power.

The Army of Irminsul made camp on top of a hill looking down into a valley below with many boulders, escarpments and ridges that made it look as if a giant had scooped up a handful of earth and flung it down carelessly. One particularly long and wide ridge between six and seven feet high lay near the center of the valley. It was not visible from the hill, as a large clump of trees grew there and obscured it from view. They always camped with their back to the Silver City so that their precious supply lines, their one major advantage, could not be cut off, for parties of enemy raiders could not break through their lines. If they ever were cut off from their supply lines, the price it would eventually cost the Army of Irminsul would be the very war itself. Rothgaric could not allow that to happen.

The night before the battle, Léofric lay in his tent, trying fruitlessly to sleep. The entire camp was as silent except for the occasional quiet hooting of an owl or low croaking of a frog, yet some restless anxiety tugged at his heart, proving it impossible to rest, for his mind was disquieted and restless. After several hours of tossing and turning, Léofric finally decided to seek refuge out under the starry sky. He arose, threw about his shoulders the wolfskin cloak that Surgessar had made for him, and walked silently out into the night, walking very slowly and avoiding sticks and brambles so as to make no sound that could possibly wake those sleeping quietly in their tents.

As Léofric pulled it on, he noticed a strange look in the wolf's death-frozen eyes, a look of uncertainty and timidity. Perhaps the young wolf, barely risen from cubhood, had been struggling to prove himself, to find his place in the world.

The stars, twinkling brilliantly in the dark curtain of night, seemed to glare at him like angelic prophets foretelling misfortune. He walked a short distance down the hill and laid his head on a small stone. Inhaling deeply of the cool night air, having not been able to sleep for several hours, he was soon fast asleep.

First bright, then dull colors filled his sleep-needy mind. They danced, blurred and mixed haphazardly in front of his eyes. His body felt detached from reality, as if it were floating somewhere out of the realm of thought and time. Slowly the colors took the shape of the tall trees on the hill. As his subconscious eyes watched them, their branches became pointed and sharp. As he watched longer, these pointed edges turned from wood to steel and became the blades of pikes. These were swung level by invisible hands.

Then he saw armored stallions, the warhorses of Irminsul, charging underneath the pikes. He felt their hot breath and beating hooves as they came. The fear was plainly visible in their wide, frenzied eyes. Mail leggings stained with blood trailed behind many of the stirrups. Many of the saddles were bloody as well, and the many cries of the wounded and dying echoed in his ears. He saw Halifar's good battle axe lying bloodied. A horse which he had seen mighty Halifar ride on the march seemed to be almost on top of Léofric, when suddenly the boy's eyes opened to find the bluish pink light of an early spring morning slowly beginning to illuminate the wide sky above him.

The pink rays of dawn were reaching up over the horizon as Léofric stood to his feet. What could the dream mean? Could he have been sword dreaming? No. That could not be the answer. It had been too obscure. Nothing like that could ever possibly happen!

He had obviously eaten too much venison the night before. Turning, he walked back to camp for breakfast.

After quickly downing a bowl of broth, Léofric went to the royal tent, where his father and the captains were discussing the plan of attack. A tall man with graying black hair pointed down at the map with a gloved hand.

"We outnumber the enemy. If we charge directly down the hill, we shall have the momentum of the incline, and the shock of our attack shall be too much for them to bear. Those not skewered by our lances shall flee back to their camp, causing pandemonium as they reach it. This will give us a chance to rout the entire regiment."

Rothgaric nodded approvingly. "Good. Halifar, you shall lead the charge."

Tendrils of doubt touched Léofric's mind. Part of his conscience was urging him to tell the military council of his dream. And yet, if he were wrong, he would prove himself to be lax and ineffective, and endanger the lives of many brave men. He finally decided that his father was accustomed to war and tactics and would surely not need him on this occasion.

Pikemen dressed in the blackened mail of the rebels stood atop the ridge in the center of the valley. Jarkin, their captain, shaded his eyes with a mailed hand beneath his kettle helmet. He leaned to the right.

Horsemen in gleaming mail were forming ranks on the hill. Jarkin looked back over his shoulder. Gollmorn's cavalry was seemingly ready to meet them. Perfect. Everything was going according to plan. He would finally have his vengeance on the upstart page that stole his captaincy.

He looked back at his two score men who had been specially selected for this mission. "The enemy is preparing to charge. Be ready!"

Atop the hill, the black-bearded Halifar was mounted before the cavalry, his good single-bladed axe in his left hand and the reins in his right. A round steel cap with mail skirting was on his head. Turning to Léofric, he smiled broadly and said, "Today is my little son's sixth birthday. You both are alike in spirit. Perhaps I will have a treasure from the enemy camp to bring back to him when the war is over. He is probably eating his mother's famous lamb stew even as we speak. I think he should very much like to trade places with you and be away at war, rather than at home. He does not realize, in his young naivety, the value of living in peace. Ah, well. Little boys will always be little boys, I suppose. It is time for me to go. I shall see you after the victory, my friend."

Swinging his axe forward to denote the order to charge, he thundered down the hill at the head of his cavalry. As they gained momentum, the mailed horsemen swung their lances level.

Seeing their enemy advance, the rebel cavalry swung their lances level. The ground shook with the thundering of hooves. The two forces of armored horse drew closer and closer. The forces of Irminsul kept their eyes on the enemy before them with rapt intensity, not looking to the right or the left. When both were still several yards away from each other, disaster befell the cavalry of Irminsul.

At precisely the planned moment, the enemy pikemen on the ridge swung their pikes level. Halifar's cavalry were riding too rapidly to notice before it was too late. Many were unhorsed and those who were not were killed by the sheer force of the blow could not even stand before they were dispatched by keen enemy pike blades.

The pikemen jumped off the ridge and ran the unhorsed through while the enemy cavalry stopped and slashed and hacked the defenseless men to pieces. Only one man out of the whole unfortunate lot had the strength to defend himself. Bold Halifar, his leg trapped under his fallen horse, swung his axe wildly at his assailants, surprisingly cutting down many. At last, a well-armored rebel horseman who had galloped up to join in the slaughter was able to drive his spear through the brave man's heart. With his last breath, the courageous fighter looked up at the sky and thought of his little boy and wife whom he would never see again in this life. His trusted battle axe fell from his mailed hand. There lay the mighty Halifar, his many foes lying slain about him.

Jarkin, the captain of the rebel pikemen, smiled wickedly as he saw Halifar die. He congratulated himself on being the instrument of this man's death, for it was his men who had struck down the raven-haired warrior. Jarkin thought of him as a trophy he had won in this war. His death was a prize of the greatest possible vengeance. Smirking, he went to report the victory to Gollmorn. In his selfish, devious mind, he hoped his success would give him a promotion, perhaps even a generalship. His mind was lost in his dreams of glory as he returned to camp.

The cavalry of Irminsul was defeated. Léofric was beside himself with grief. The strange vision had been a sword dream, and it had come true, terribly true. Halifar had prematurely joined the mighty hosts of old, the deeds of whom he had sung so often. He would not be ashamed to ride in their vast, noble company, for though he was young, his virtuous deeds were many.

Thinking quickly, Surgessar spurred his horse and galloped down into the valley, retrieving Halifar's axe from where it lay on the bloody ground, thus preventing one of the enemy from stealing it for a prize, whispering a blessing for his slain friend as he turned his horse about and returned to camp.

Rothgaric, seeing the disaster unfold before his eyes, quickly came to understand the enemy's dastardly stratagem. He pounded his great fist into his hand and uttered a cry of desperate frustration. "How could this happen? If only it wasn't for those infernal trees. Halifar, brave friend Halifar, I shall avenge you, I swear it. You shall be honored in songs and tales from this day until the ending of the world."

Léofric went alone to his tent and wept bitterly. How could he have been so stupid? Now the valley ran red with the blood of the King's men. He had told himself that he would endanger the lives of many brave men if he spoke of his dream, but by not doing so, he had caused their deaths. A brave captain's blood was on his hands! His dear friend, the one who had made camp life agreeable and lighthearted, was now gone forever. His poor widow and now fatherless son would never see him again.

Drying his tears, Léofric went to the royal tent to find his father and Surgessar. The captains were conferring with the King over the next course of action, pouring worriedly over maps and charts.

Clearing his throat, Léofric said, "Pardon me, my King, but I must speak with you and Surgessar alone. It is urgent."

"Very well," said Rothgaric, taking his leave of his captains.

The three returned to Léofric's tent. Falling on his knees before his father, Léofric said humbly, "Father, I must beg your forgiveness. Last night, I dreamed of the disaster that transpired today. I neglected to tell you, for I was unsure of what I saw. I told myself you were accustomed to war and tactics and that I knew nothing. Forgive me, I beg you."

Rothgaric was flabbergasted. "Son, why did you not inform us of this? Had you told us of your vision, the blood of many valiant men, and the blood of the valiant Halifar, whom I loved as a brother, would not stain the valley below us. You are Sword Dreamer and you must perform your duty," he seethed, trying to hold back his visible anger and extreme disappointment. He turned and left without saying more. His words had cut his son deep like a dagger, and only served to make Léofric's guilt all the more unbearable. Léofric stared at the ground blankly, unable to speak, overwhelmed by his relentless grief.

Surgessar laid a hand on the young man's shoulder. "Take today's defeat as a terrible but valuable lesson. You must hone your skills and your perception of dreams. No matter how bizarre the dream, you must never be afraid to tell us, for any dream may be of import to the war. You are the Sword Dreamer, as your father says. I do not foresee failure as your destiny."

The elf left. Léofric, exhausted by the trauma of the day's defeat, fell back on his cot and after thrashing and turning repeatedly, eventually fell into a deep but troubled sleep. As he wandered in the halls of unconsciousness, Halifar's dying battle cries reached his ears. He knew, even in sleep, that the brave captain's blood was forever on his hands. He felt as if he had lost the brother that he never had, and it stung his soul like a scorpion's sharp, poisonous sting. He would never hear the songs of old sung with such joy ever again. He wept, even in sleep, for the loss of his dear comrade.

SEVEN

THE DOLDRUMS IN THE WINDS OF WAR

About a week after the disastrous cavalry charge, Léofric awoke and walked out of his tent into the brightening dawn. Pinkish light illuminated the awakening sky and a light breeze blew along the plain. Although it was only about the sixth hour of the morning, the camp was already alive with activity. Men sat outside their tents, sharpening their swords and stirring pots of meager soup for breakfast. Others downed mugs of watered down ale to shake the tiredness from their minds. Several of them leaned listlessly on the poles that supported the stew pots cooking over the fires, but lately come as they were from the world of dreams. The sheep, pigs and cattle bleated, squealed and lowed for their food as they awoke in their pins. Mist wafted down from the mountains and was painted gold by the rising sun.

Léofric went to the royal tent. There, he found his father with the captains of the Army. They were conferring over the yellowed map set on a large wooden dais around which they huddled intently. The yellowed parchment showed the northern regions of Irminsul, hemmed in by the semicircle of the northern, northwestern and northeastern Kjartens. Léofric entered quietly, but the men were so concentrated on their discussion that they seemed to take no note of him as he walked into the tent.

"A large portion of Gollmorn's army has moved to the north," said a flaxen-haired commander, pointing a mailed finger to a spot north of the camp; where the land began to slope up toward the northwestern foothills of the Kjartens "If we stay here, we run the risk of being killed at a distance by his longbowmen. I believe we should move at least a league to the north. There, we can be prepared to repel any attack the enemy can devise."

Rothgaric thought for a time. At length, he said, "You are right, Maelthaen. Issue the order to break camp. We ride north."

"But, my lord," said another, "it has only been a week since the disastrous battle, if it can even be called a battle, for it was a slaughter. The men have not had enough time for adequate rest. Delay the march for at least a week. Then, the men will be well-rested and we will have received fresh supplies from the Silver City."

The man who said this was Kirlúnd, the tall, loyal captain who had been commander of the infantry before the rebellion, when that force was sizable. When most of his men had followed Gollmorn, the seasoned infantry commander had remained loyal to Futhark.

He was clad in silver-gray mail, and a long cape of heavy brown fur that he wore even in the summertime hung from his shoulders. At his waist hung a hand-and-a-half falchion, a unicorn emblazoned in silver on its dark, curved scabbard.

His short black hair and beard were flecked with patches of white, evidence of his advancing age. However, his shoulders were still broad and powerful. His brown eyes often betrayed bravery and battle courage, but also showed a strong sense of caution.

"The longer we stay here, Commander Kirlúnd," replied Rothgaric confidently, "the more chance the enemy has to attack. We must leave this place. We have no other choice. The enemy will have discovered our weak points in time. Maelthaen, give the order to break camp. We ride north."

The horses were once again saddled. The tents were taken down, the livestock herded and the baggage train filled. This was done quickly so as to thwart any possible surprise attacks by the enemy. The Army then set out at a steady pace.

Léofric felt a deep emptiness as he rode Haldor that morning, a profound sadness the source of which he could not discern. Finally, he discovered the wellspring of his melancholy. Halifar was not with them. The raven-haired giant had always been quick to laugh and talk amiably. It was he who had made the march pass so quickly, with his trumpeter's voice singing of the great deeds of the mighty men of old, and now he was gone forever, all because the Sword Dreamer had neglected his duty. Léofric fell silent with grief as he thought of this. The sky seemed gray and overcast, as if even the very heavens were mourning the valiant warrior.

As the Army neared the mountains, the road became rougher and the pace slowed considerably. Very often the baggage carts were stuck in ruts, the pages straining their backs as they attempted to pry the large wheels free with long wooden staves. Gravel found its way into the horses' hooves on more than a few occasions, slowing their pace all the more. Delays such as these caused many of the captains to become irritable. The common soldiers' spirits were saved only by the good food that continued to come in from Auraheim. There was one benefit that their enemy had had no success in taking from them: their invaluable, uninterrupted supply lines. The men would have been much more cheery, even without the copious good food, had joyous Halifar been with them. He had never allowed anything, no matter how serious, to dampen his spirits.

The Army of Irminsul set up camp several leagues from the base of the northwestern Kjartens. Scattered trees, shrubs and clumps of green grass grew among the tall golden stalks of plains grass. The green blades nodded their heads toward the mountains as the breeze rustled past them. Very often winds blew up from the south, seeming to carry war news. Scouts reported very slow movement from the enemy in the north.

For two fortnights no decisive action was taken, and, as a result, everyone in the camp became anxious. Spirits were also worsened by damp, rainy spring weather at night, often followed by oppressively humid days. Though no one spoke of it outside the military councils, the extreme anxiety was plainly visible in their eyes. Even Surgessar, patient and methodical though he was, was slightly unnerved by the lack of action. He often sat in front of his tent, sharpening his scimitar or oiling his crossbow, whistling Elvish lays through his teeth. He did not speak to anyone save Rothgaric, and when others ventured to say something to him, he answered in only one or two curt words.

His daughter seemed to hold up better than he. She would hold fencing bouts with Léofric, as Rothgaric was now too busy with his kingly duties to spend his time in pursuits such as teaching his son how to better defend himself. In truth, the only time Léofric spent with his father was composed of meetings in the royal tent with the captains of the Army. These times were not intended for father-son bonding, yet Léofric enjoyed them, having been bereft of his father all of his life.

The beautiful dark Elven girl's style of fencing was entirely new to Léofric, as he had never fought an adversary who used two swords. It was very different from fighting with a hand-and-a-half broadsword. She struck quickly, as a serpent strikes, often hooking his sword in the back of her blade and pulling it from his hands.

"You must parry from both directions," she would say, after she had once again knocked his broadsword from his hands, laughing sympathetically at his clumsiness.

Once, after a lesson was over and Léofric and Súndéa were resting, Léofric said, "I long for the day when I can fight in battle."

"No Sword Dreamer has ever fought before. He is too valuable to risk his life."

"What?" He looked both shocked and disappointed. He had hoped that his new life in the Army would afford him a chance for adventure and battle glory. Now all his hopes and dreams had been dashed to pieces in one fell instant.

She laid a gentle, loving hand on his arm. "There is a first time for everything, my dear, strong-hearted warrior. Perhaps you will fight someday. We are all part of the battle for the fate of the world that rages all around us, and it is greater than any of the wars and battles of men or elves. You are an important part of that battle. A great gift and weapon with the potential of righteous power is yours, for you are the Sword Dreamer. For years the Army of

Irminsul has been caught in the mire of despair, but you have given them hope, and that is one of the greatest weapons of all. For now, do as my father says and hone your skills as the Sword Dreamer. Then you shall bring us victory. Do not fret. It shall come to pass. Not all honor is won in battle."

EIGHT

THE WILD RIDER

As the state of affairs continued on without adventure, Léofric longed for action, or at least a useful way to pass the time. He could not spend all the copious idle hours studying swordplay. He longed to talk to Surgessar, for, ever since he met him, Léofric had greatly desired to talk with him of Elven lore. But as the dark elf's mood was worsening for the lack of military action, the boy had not dared to speak to him.

One day however, he saw the elf grooming his mount and singing softly to the stallion in Elvish. Walking slowly over to where Surgessar sat, Léofric cautiously said, "Good morrow, friend. You have never told me the name of this fine beast."

"His name is Maelros," Surgessar replied absent-mindedly, not looking up from his task. "He is named for and descended from the first horse Gildéador ever created."

"Please, tell me his tale. Of the first Maelros, I mean."

Surgessar looked up and laughed. "The tale of Maelros is also the tale of Frékanéor, his rider, and it is so great a tale, it hardly needs me to tell it." Surgessar cleared his throat and put down the brush. Léofric sat down on the ground next to him and listened intently.

"In the days when the world was young, not long after the awakening of the elves, who are the elder children of Gildéador, the first potentates of the Elvenlands marched often to do battle with the forces of the Dark Enemy. In those days there were no horses, and thus no cavalry. The infantry of the Elven princes were hard-pressed against the forces of the Dark Enemy in every battle, and lost many men to his swift, dark fire worms.

"There was a powerful elf ruler named Laeglam. He was named for the stout, sharp spears that he and his men used most effectively in battle. He had but one son, whom he named Oromandos. This prince was courageous in battle and passing handsome.

"One night in midsummer, during which time the Dark Enemy's power was weakest and the Elven armies rested, Oromandos walked over the grassy hills under the night sky, beseeching Gildéador for some weapon, some aid with which his people could have victory over the Dark Enemy.

"Gildéador heard his cry and saw that it was not good for him to be alone in the fight. So there appeared before the prince a magnificent creature, such as he had never seen before. It was a stallion, though he knew not what to call it. Its coat and mane were as white as pearl, its legs strong and powerful. Oromandos was awe-struck.

"In the silence of the night, Gildéador spoke to the prince's mind and told him to leap upon the creature's back. Just as Oromandos was about to do so, the Dark Enemy sent his servant, the black rook Auglum, to alight on the horse's shoulder.

"The fell bird whispered an evil song into the stallion's ear and flew away, cawing wickedly. Immediately, the horse's hide turned from white to black and its mind was given over to madness. Its eyes fumed red like fire, the mad song of the wicked bird echoing in its ears.

"When Oromandos endeavored to mount the crazed beast, the horse bucked and threw him soundly to the ground. Oromandos stood, a righteous rage burning like blue fire in his eyes.

"He exclaimed, 'Though it kills me, I will drive this madness from you.'

"With a wild yell, he leaped upon the stallion's back and dug his fingernails deep into the mount's hide. The mad stallion shot across the hills faster than a ballista bolt fired from one of the war machines of the Dark Enemy. Oromandos was forced to quickly doff his hauberk and throw off his sword in its baldric. He cried aloud all the healing magic he knew, but to no avail. Because the beast would not listen, he shouted louder and louder until his voice reached a screaming crescendo. In order to keep his weight light and not fall from his mad mount, he shed his cloak, and everything but his trousers and leather boots.

"Through the summer and fall and on through the winter, he rode on that wild ride. Nothing else mattered to him now. His mind was consumed with rage. Not the unholy, selfish rage that consumes Gollmorn, but the pure, righteous anger that Gildéador had given to his heart.

"His hair grew long and wild and was blotched by rain and mud. He would have also grown a long, unruly beard had he been a man and not an elf. Every time he neared a town or city, the people would hear his wild cries rolling ahead of him across the plain and flee in terror. Frékanéor they called him, the wild rider. For a time, Oromandos even forgot his own name in his rage.

"With the coming of spring, as the first buds emerged on the cold, damp trees, Gildéador spoke to Oromandos' distressed mind. He gave the prince the proper word to speak, and Oromandos, his hope returning, shouted hoarsely, 'Glasta!' This word later came to mean 'peace' and is still used to halt all Elven horses, for the stallions of the Elvenlands understand the high speech of the elves, their masters.

"At the sound of that word, the stallion halted. The mad look left its eyes. Its coat became snow white again.

"Gildéador looked down and said, 'I am proud of you, my son, Wild Rider.' Then he created a mate for the stallion. Oromandos remembered his lost identity. Then he went back to his land, father and people and the name he gave to the stallion was Maelros. He had become the first horseman in Éalindé. He himself changed his name to Frékanéor and rode Maelros to many victories against the Dark Enemy. He bred many stallions for the soldiers of his army to ride. He adapted his father's spear tactics to also become the first horseman to bear a lance. Descended from the union of Maelros and his mate come all the horses that are alive today. Laeglam was greatly pleased with his son, and by his brave leadership, the realm of his House increased. Frékanéor dwelt till the end of his days in the green lands north of the northern Kjartens. He bore a great rectangular golden shield into battle that his father had his smiths make for him to commemorate his returning. It had a shining green stone for the central boss. He bore it to many victories. He named his realm Gladdéas, 'Fields of Emerald'. It is from him that the mighty Nilmeron claimed heritage. After the brave Nilmeron won the Battle of the Foothills and became King of Irminsul, Gladdéas was renamed Nilmeronel, 'Land of Nilmeron'. It was in that green, fertile land that I was born. The golden shield of Frékanéor can still be seen on the battle standard of Nilmeronel to this very day.

"After the coming of men, the younger children of Gildéador, horses found their way south of the Kjartens into the lands that would become Irminsul, the land of men. Most of these horses forgot the speech of elves with the passing of time, except a select few. Most of these few, noble stallions have coats as snow white as that of their noble ancestor.

"When Frékanéor died in battle, he was laid to rest beside Maelros, the horse which his courageous heart had tamed."

Léofric sat there for a moment, awestruck at what he had heard. At length, he said, "Thank you for sharing some of the lore of your people with me, my friend. That was a truly amazing story. I am always astounded at the deep knowledge and wisdom with which Gildéador has gifted your people."

From that day forward, Léofric never looked at his stallion Haldor as merely a simple beast again.

The next day at about the twelfth hour, Léofric was near the smithy section of the camp, eating a small loaf of bread for his midday meal and watching some of the weapon smiths at their work. Captain Maelthaen and his long time mount, Beornost, were also in the smithy section of the camp. Maelthaen was waiting while his roan charger's hooves were being re-shod. Horse and rider were standing next to an anvil which happened, because of lethargy on the part of the smith, to be piled high with weapons as well as set off center on its small iron table. These weapons also were by no means just small daggers. Broadswords, heavy battle axes, maces and spears, all of the heaviest steel, were piled high on the off-center iron anvil. This caused it to unnoticeably begin to teeter like the sign outside an inn on a windy day, creaking on its chains. But its movement was so slight, that not even Léofric noticed it. The anvil swayed somewhat on its center of gravity for a moment, unheeded.

Suddenly, the anvil could manage the pull of gravity no longer. It fell with a low resounding thud, pinning Beornost's leg to the ground and scattering weapons everywhere with a clanking crash. Everyone there heard the dull crunch of bone as the large block of iron hit the poor horse's leg. Luckily, the smith was able to dodge out of the path of the falling block of iron, and none of the falling blades had struck either the blond captain or his unfortunate mount. The poor roan beast neighed piteously in agonizing pain.

Maelthaen, somewhat frenzied by the sudden emergency, soon recovered and took charge of the situation. To the smith, he ordered, "Run quickly. Find Surgessar! Tell him we need him immediately." He began to sweat, and rubbed his temples madly as he waited in an endeavor to calm himself. The fair-haired, strong captain had ridden that same stallion since his elevation to captaincy and it was very dear to him. He could not bear to see Beornost in such excruciating pain and terror.

Surgessar soon came running, his lips still stained from the bowl of beef broth he had been drinking when the smith found him. The wind of his running was like a gale upon the Elverean Sea. Kneeling by the fallen stallion, he began singing softly to it in Elvish. "Glastoné, é allonín, glastoné, é allonín." He repeated this refrain many times in a rhythmic, soothing tone. Everyone in the immediate area seemed to feel comforted and at peace when the beautiful Elvish song reached their ears. Even Maelthaen ceased to sweat and the anxious look left his eyes.

Slowly, as steadily as a violent rainstorm abates, the panic left the stallion's eyes and its breathing became steadier. It ceased to struggle. The elves truly had a deep understanding of horses, for, as Surgessar had said, the first horseman had been an elf. Everyone in the vicinity also seemed to be calmed and stopped, almost spellbound by the beautiful, soothing Elvish song. It seemed to Léofric that Gildéador took pleasure in the song.

"What is going on?" asked a slightly gruff voice. Maelthaen looked up to see Kettil, who had come to discover the cause of all the noise. Maelthaen quickly informed him of all that had happened.

"Well, that problem is easily remedied," said the bald, muscular smith. "Keep the beast calm so he will not move, Surgessar."

With that, the short man knelt down, wrapped his corded arms around the anvil, and lifted it up with as much ease as if it had been a small wooden crate, not even breaking a sweat. Léofric stared, disbelievingly. The anvil must have weighed at least six hundred pounds and would have taken six full-grown men to lift. What was more, Kettil appeared to be a man of at least fifty years of age.

Léofric was even more amazed when the old smith hooked his arms under Beornost's belly and began carrying the full-grown stallion to the surgeons' tent to have its leg mended. Léofric did not know what to think. No man could lift a heavy anvil single-handedly, much less a full-grown war stallion. Apparently there was more to the old smith then he had at first supposed.

That evening at dinner, Léofric sought out Surgessar to question him about what had happened earlier. The dark-skinned Elven warrior was sitting off by himself, sopping up the last of his soup with a chunk of rye bread.

"Truly, friend," Léofric said invitingly, "I know a little of the magic of elves and the high ways of your people, but what transpired today with Maelthaen's horse was truly amazing. It was as if you were speaking into the stallion's very soul."

"Oh, but I was. Or, you could say that it was something of the sort. The King That Is has imbued the language that he created for my people with the power to soothe the soul of beast, elf, dwarf and man alike. When we perform a service that He has laid out for us to do, or use our gifts to honor Him, His pleasure fills our hearts.

"Somewhat similar to the soothing of horses, as you saw me do today, mothers in all the kingdoms of the Elvenlands use like songs to calm the spirits of their babes. In the memory of my heart, I can still hear my mother singing songs to me as she held me in arms shortly after I was born. Often in the past I have recalled her beautiful voice on the night before battle, and it gives comfort and courage to my mind and spirit.

"After Súndéa's mother died, it was left to me to comfort my daughter during such times as best I could. Ah," he sighed wistfully, "If only my fair Negiatha had been there to train and bring up her daughter as only a loving mother can. But, Gildéador knows the proper time to bring us home, and it is not wise to question His plan. I have watched over and protected my daughter all her life." He laid a hand on Léofric's shoulder, and looked deep into his eyes. "It is a responsibility that I recommend highly, Sword Dreamer. No young suitors of my race capture her heart, but she loves you very much.

And so do I, my friend. So do I." Léofric was somewhat surprised, yet exceedingly glad to hear that his mentor put so much confidence in him and he smiled thankfully. Despite the struggles and darkness, there was much light for which to be thankful.

NINE

THE ELVEN DECEPTION

About a month after the Army settled, Léofric was in his tent, suffering another sleepless night. He tossed and turned for hours to no avail. His forehead was hot and sweaty, yet he was not ill. Every time he closed his eyes, his efforts at sleep would become more futile. The camp was deathly quiet, yet his heart pounded loudly in his ears like a kettle drum. How he envied the other men with their seemingly effortless, refreshing sleep. He turned over and punched his pillow once again.

Finally he decided that the cool night air would do him good. He left his tent and walked to a small tree several yards from his tent and lay down on the soft heather-studded grass. The stars twinkled brightly, as if they were trying to tell him something important. He closed his eyes and felt his consciousness melt away.

The mists of a deep, profound unconsciousness began to envelope his weary mind. Before his eyes appeared an ocean of light and color, swirling and indiscernible. Slowly, out of the chaos, he began to discern images, somewhat blanketed in a light mist, before his closed eyes. He saw the camp of the Army of Irminsul. It stood empty but for a few guards. A small group of tall mail-clad riders with pointed ears and long flowing hair were riding up toward the vacant camp from the southwest. He could not make out the insignia on their surcoats, for they kept them hidden, seemingly by intention. He watched, horrified, as the few guards that remained in camp were mercilessly put to the sword. How could elves bring themselves to do this? Elves were by nature a merciful and kind race, allies of the King. Here they were acting as butchers. They, by their code of honor, had always held the lives of all the free peoples as most sacred, be they Elvish, human or of another free race. How could this be?

Léofric awoke suddenly in a cold sweat. This had most certainly been a sword dream. He could not afford to doubt his intuition. He could not fail to report. He jumped to his feet and ran straightaway to the royal tent, to report to his father and the captains of the Army.

He burst in as the King, Surgessar and the other captains were conferring over the map, as they had done repeatedly over the last month.

"I have seen it," Léofric shouted as he raced into the tent unannounced. The mail-clad men looked up suddenly, obviously displeased at the unexpected interruption.

"I have had a sword dream, my King. I am certain of it. I came here to report it immediately after I awoke. I have just come from my tent."

"What was it, Sword Dreamer?" Surgessar asked, looking at him intently.

"It was very strange. It did not make much sense to my mind. I saw our camp, empty but for a few guards. I saw elves riding from the southwest to attack it."

Silence followed this explanation. Léofric noticed several of the captains trying to hide their bewilderment and disbelief. Finally, Rothgaric said, "As much as I would like to believe you, I simply cannot. It is impossible that the elves could attack us from the southwest, as the Elvenlands lie north of the northern Kjartens. The elves, especially the elves of Nilmeronel, have been our allies for many centuries. Also, no elves have come across the mountains since the beginning of the war. No, Sword Dreamer, you must be mistaken."

Léofric felt quite abashed at this rejection. He felt that they were making a terrible mistake that he felt would cost valiant men their lives. Why would they not listen to him? Was he not the Sword Dreamer?

The captains were just about to turn back to their calculations when a scout entered the tent. His mail-clad breast was heaving and his face was red and sweaty from hours of riding. "Enemy cavalry," he panted, "riding down from the north. Thousands of them. If we tarry in taking action, the camp will surely be razed to the ground."

Rothgaric thought for a moment. For a time he seemed almost to waver, debating silently within his mind whether to believe his son or his seasoned military instinct. Then he said decisively, "We shall take every able-bodied horse and crush them!"

The war horns of Irminsul sounded and the armored cavalry rode out to meet that of Gollmorn. The enemy was quick in coming;

so quick that the two forces met not a hundred yards from the camp of the King. Léofric rode in the rear where he would not be harmed.

The forces of Gollmorn did not offer much resistance and soon many of the enemy riders were being forced to retreat, most of their number having been felled by the mighty, flashing swords of the red-bearded man and his valiant captains. The enemy cavalry knew their mission and Gollmorn had made it very clear that failure was an offense punishable by death.

Rothgaric's cavalry soon bellowed a loud exultation and began to give chase. The rebel cavalry spurred their mounts anxiously, careful to keep just out of reach of the death-dealing swords and lances of Rothgaric's exuberant men.

Surgessar wondered at the apparent ease of the impending victory. He sensed movement out of the corner of his eye and looked back over his shoulder at the camp.

His keen Elven eyes saw something that chilled his blood. The forces of Irminsul had taken every horse they had to counter the enemy, yet a handful of riders were among the tents!

He yelled to Rothgaric over the din. "I must take a few men back to camp. There are strange horsemen in the camp. It is urgent. I must go now."

Rothgaric nodded his approval, looking up for an instant from a rider he had unhorsed and slain. Sweat poured down his bearded face, and his broadsword was stained with blood.

Turning his horse, the dark elf beckoned men to follow him, and galloped at the head of several dozen lightly armored men back down the plain to camp. To his horror, he found several guards slain and a few of the tents looted as he ducked briefly inside. No weapons had been taken, only supplies. Apart from being ransacked, most of the tents themselves were still intact. Surgessar sensed, however, that something catastrophic had happened while they were engaged with the enemy cavalry.

One of the enemy riders galloped toward him with a cry, brandishing his sword above his head. Surgessar took careful aim with his crossbow and fired. The bolt sailed straight into the man's breast, knocking him off his horse. The riderless mount galloped off and the elf did not have time to pay it any heed, for he was anxious to uncover the strange mystery. The rider lay still on his back, the bolt protruding from his cloak. His sword was still grasped tightly in his lifeless hand.

The dark elf dismounted and walked to the corpse. Surgessar pulled back the chestnut mane from the side of the head so he could better behold the face. The soldier was tall, with long flowing locks, and pointed ears. An elf! The Army had been attacked by his own people. They had broken the time-honored alliance with the King. But no! As Surgessar reached down to touch the ear, it broke off in his fingers. Wax! He removed the bolt and drew back the man's heavy cloak. The red falcon of Gollmorn! The charge of the enemy to the north of camp and the easy routing had all been a carefully planned ruse.

The dark elf looked up in despair and anger. "Oh, cruel trickery. Léofric's sword dream came true though we did not understand it! Now the day is lost, though we had won it by numbers slain."

He rode among the surrounding tents and caught the whiff of smoke rising from the direction of the supply tent, his keen eyes catching a dark mist billowing on the air as he neared his destination. By the time he reached it, he discovered that half the store of grain and meat had already been burned past salvaging. The flames had not reached the cloth of silver by the time he reached the tent. Thinking quickly, he doused and stamped out the flames before they reached the flammable cloth of silver, so the structure itself was saved. However, the smell of scorched meat gave a foul stench to the air.

In a blind rage, spewing angry words in Elvish at the top of his lungs, Surgessar charged to the head of his own men as they rushed through the camp, hunting down the other raiders among the tents. Several of those Surgessar happened to accost were decapitated in one blow, for great was his fury at their blatant attempt to defame his sacred race. One man endeavored to unhorse the elf with his spear, but Surgessar easily deflected the mad thrust with the flat of his blade and the same scimitar caused the man's throat to spit forth a jet of crimson as the elf dealt a red-raged stroke. Surgessar's stallion next galloped after a fleeing man, leapt in the air, and the horse's iron shod hoof came down with a crunch on the spine of the fleeing raider. The elf's eyes were wild with indignation at this "Elven deception" of the enemy and he brandished his scimitar in defiance at the decoy enemy cavalry that distracted Rothgaric's men. What fools they all had been! If only they had listened to the Sword Dreamer!

The remaining raiders fought with the desperate fury of cornered men, for they knew they were hopelessly outnumbered. The rage of the men of Irminsul paled in comparison with that of the elf, but it nevertheless gave strength to their sword arms, and soon all of the raiders were killed.

When the last of the enemy cavalry on the plain had been killed and the ruse reported to Rothgaric, the red-haired giant stood before the Army in front of the royal tent and announced, "Men of

Irminsul, the body of cavalry we slew today was sent by the enemy to draw us away from camp. Gollmorn sent raiders disguised as warriors of the Elvenlands to destroy our camp and force us to capitulate. We have lost several men and half of our food supply. Let us mourn the dead. Do not concern yourselves with the loss of our supplies, for these can be replenished from Auraheim. I shall ever regret my error, and my lack of confidence in the Sword Dreamer."

After the men had disassembled, Rothgaric called Léofric to the royal tent. Surgessar and the other captains of the Army were also present. He looked gravely and sadly at his son. "We all must humbly beg your forgiveness. We have decided that from this day forth we will always heed the counsel of the Sword Dreamer. In this, we are all of one accord."

When the captains had been sent away, Rothgaric came forward and embraced his son. "I should listen to you not only because you are the Sword Dreamer, but also because you are my son. I am very sorry, the blame rests on me. I am sorry, Léofric, for my grievous error this day. Do not lose hope, my son. We shall be victorious."

TEN

THE HORSE AND RIDER FALLS

Several days later, Léofric entered the royal tent to find that a scout had returned to report to Rothgaric and the captains of the Army. The man had ridden all night and was now seated, refreshing himself with a tankard of ale drying his sweat-drenched face with a cloth. "Gollmorn has stationed a large body of longbowmen in the foothills many leagues to the West. If we strike soon, we can eliminate them and the rebels will have precious few archers left. If we delay, we will assuredly be attacked and we do not have enough longbowmen to counter them."

Rothgaric mused silently for a moment. "You may be right." Turning to the captains, he asked, "what think you?"

"The men are getting fatigued from marching," Maelthaen countered. "If we overtax their strength, they will be useless in battle."

"But as has been said, if we stay here, we run the risk of being attacked and killed at a distance," said another.

"We will simply have to run the risk of overtiring the men," Rothgaric said after a time. "Give the order to break camp."

The day proved fair and the horses at least were well rested, so the march took only a day. As Léofric rode by the side of his father, Súndéa rode up beside him.

"Good morrow, my King," she greeted Rothgaric, inclining her head.

Turning to Léofric, she asked, "Let us fall back a few paces so we can talk in private."

When they were out of earshot of Rothgaric, she asked, "What ails you, my lord? You look as if your morning meal did not sit well with you."

Léofric drew in a deep breath. "I was asking myself why I of all people was the Sword Dreamer. I believe myself to be a failure, for I have brought my father and King no victories, only defeat. If I cannot serve my purpose, I see no hope for Irminsul."

The Elven girl smiled. "I would tell myself similar things when my father was teaching me the art of the sword. I could never seem to hold my own against him. More than once, I thought of giving up hope of ever mastering the sword and becoming a fighter. But then I resolved one day that, no matter the odds, I would become a skilled fighter, even though I was very slow, my eyes were not quick and my strokes were not smooth and fluid like those of my father. It was a decision that I had to make, for, as my mother died in childbirth, I was forced to go away to war with my father. Thus, I had to learn how to fight in order to survive. You must make a similar decision. Even though you see disaster all around you, there is the hope of a brighter future. A brighter future is what Gildéador plans for you. I know it for certain in my heart."

"Thank you for your encouraging words, my lady. They comfort me, somewhat."

Rothgaric had hired a wild man, or Vólderín, a hetman of one of the many tribes that dwelt in the cave and crag-dotted northern Kjartens, as a guide through the rocky terrain. Léofric had seen him conferring with the captains that morning as the men were breaking camp. He wore an unkempt beard and a long mane of ungroomed hair, which was bound in a topknot. His fists were as big as the head of the wooden maul he carried over his shoulder. He was clothed in a raggedy deerskin siarc and kilt, and went barefoot. He stooped forward as he walked, because he had lived all his life stooping into caves and crags in the mountain on feet that were nearly as big as bear claws, and were covered with large tufts of sweaty, scraggly brown hair. The nails of his toes grew long and yellow. His legs were fat and stocky and his gangly arms dangled near his feet as he walked. Tattoos of blue woad were etched all along his hairy arms and on what little bare skin was around his eyes and nose. He now walked near the front of the line by Rothgaric's horse. He did not trust horses and refused to mount.

Léofric trotted up beside Surgessar. "Who is that man?" he asked, indicating the wild man.

"That is Khrua-Hadrim, a Vólderín hetman of the northern Kjartens. His manners are wanting, but he is an excellent tracker."

"How does my father know him?"

"On the way back across the Kjartens from the forest of Bjor, while on his way back to the Southlands to find your mother, your father stumbled into Khrua-Hadrim's cave on a stormy night, having lost his way in the downpour. There, he found it necessary to prove himself in combat without weapons, for the Vólderín men are suspicious of all strangers, especially those bearing weapons of steel. He defended himself bravely, and since then there has been something of an unspoken, mutual understanding between them."

"How was my father able to defend himself?"

"Your father was forced to doff his armor, to even the scales. This he did willingly, being an honorable fighter. They circled the fire, eyeing each other furtively, arms dangling wildly at their sides like venomous snakes. Then the wild man lunged at your father. They rolled across the floor of the cave, casting dust on the fire, extinguishing it as they rolled past it. They grappled in the darkness for what seemed like hours, neither one gaining the upper hand. Then your father seized him by the throat in the dark, and with his other mighty hand cuffed him so great a blow that it knocked him out cold. Your father could have taken the chance to kill him. But instead, he rekindled the fire, and taking water from his water skin, brought the barbarian back to consciousness. Khrua-Hadrim's hate and distrust of the men of the south was in no way lessened by this encounter. But, as the Vólderíns value physical prowess as the defining trait of a good man, he was filled with a little of what we might call respect, in his own fashion, for your father from that night on.

"When he heard tell of a red warrior with an army needing to find safe passage to the foothills, he knew it to be your father. So he came down and offered his services, for a boon, of course."

"How do you know so much of that battle?"

"Your father and I fought and bled for years side by side. He was recruited shortly after I came into the Army as a mercenary. I took him under my wing and taught him all that I had learned from my father, Almiras the warrior, of Elven swordsmanship. Ah, times were simpler then. I was one of the first ones he told when he returned to camp before going to the Southlands."

For some strange reason, Léofric decided to make the wild man's acquaintance. He had heard strange tales of the mountain folk, but he had never seen one. Curiosity of the man who had fought his father propelled him to speak with the Vólderín, though, in truth, the man seemed in no mood to talk.

"Good morrow," said Léofric invitingly, riding up beside the tracker. The Vólderín merely grunted and did not turn, keeping his eyes on the road.

"I am called Léofric, son of Rothgaric. I hear your name is Khrua-Hadrim. I am glad to have you as an ally."

Khrua made a rumbling sound in his throat, and grunted, "Khrua no ally of men in shiny clothes! Huum bura huum! South men no care about Vólderín. Elf folk come over mountains on flying beasts. Blacken sky. Scare deer and rabbits. South men no do anything to help."

"But the elves are our friends and allies, the wisest of all the free races."

"Khrua not like elf folk. No like magic. Elf folk no care about Vólderín. Huma! Ghash huma!"

Léofric could easily see the futility of continuing the conversation, so he rode on and left the wild man to his own ruminations.

On the second day of the march, as they neared the foothills, a strange meeting took place. Khrua-Hadrim was thumping along at his usual ape-like gait, when he stopped suddenly in his tracks, immediately becoming tense and rigid, as if he were listening for voices on the air.

Suddenly, a deep-throated cry broke the silence. It sounded something like "Gham gha gha har la la!" These strange ululations sounded somewhat like words to Léofric. Barbaric words, but words nonetheless.

Suddenly, a band of about twenty short men burst out from behind one of the rock outcroppings in front of Khrua. They were all clad in mail of mediocre quality, strangely dyed to a dark, forest green color. They wore gray cloaks of rabbit's fur and each man had a bushy dark beard. They were all armed either with great spiked mauls or long-shafted battle axes that were nearly as tall as they. Their leader was the tallest among them, though he only stood about five and one-half feet in height. He had painted his eyelids with coal black war paint, and all the skin on the level of his eyelids was likewise painted black. He, like the rest of his men, had brown eyes, scraggly hair and a bushy ebon beard splotched with gray. He bore with him a maul of green steel with a single sharp back spike. He was wide of girth, though he still appeared very powerful. Unlike the Vólderín, he stood erect. He came forward and embraced Khrua, speaking guttural Vólderín gibberish in a rapid, deep tone.

Surgessar stared, as if he could not comprehend what he saw. "I thought they had passed into legend."

"Who are they?" asked Léofric, wondering at their somewhat crude, yet noble and warlike appearances.

"They are the Vuldervogund, the wild rangers of the mountains. They undoubtedly have Vólderín blood in their veins, though no one knows exactly where they originated. They learned metalworking from the men of northern Irminsul, becoming far inferior in the quality of their craft soonafter. However, the mail is useful to them as protection against the huge ravenous wolves and bears that dwell in the lonely caves throughout the Kjartens. It also disguises them when they hide among the trees and moss-covered rocks of the mountains when hunting game for food. No one has seen any of them in this land for generations."

"How do they dye the mail and weapons green?" asked Léofric.

"I am a warrior, not a weapon smith. But I have heard tell that up in the mountains, there grows here and there the vibrantly green Héarundas plant, a soft twig akin to mistletoe. The elementary craftsmen of the Vuldervogund rangers gather the twigs they can find, dry them, and then, in their crude smithies when the hot iron glows red as the setting sun, throw the twigs upon the hot metal and beat it soundly with a stout forging hammer. I have heard that this makes their weapons a little more sturdy and resilient in battle. It is considered a sign of status for a Vólderín to have a weapon of Vuldervogund make, for the giant ash war clubs and spears of the wild men are even more inferior to good shining Irminsul steel than the crude green steel weapons of the mountain rangers."

Léofric left the dark elf, and rode up to where the Vuldervogund chieftain was meeting with Rothgaric. The wild warrior spoke slowly, though he had more complete powers of human speech than his Vólderín friend.

"I am Dunndag Greenmail. Am last chieftain of the Vuldervogund rangers. Ghan-Haradul, Khrua's father, was friend of mine. Have promised to follow Khrua
 in quest for vengeance. If Khrua aid King of Irminsul, I aid King of Irminsul."

The foothills of the Kjartens seemed small mountains unto themselves. They stood out, fertile and green, dotted with jagged boulders and stones up and down their slopes. The Army would have been lost long among them were it not for the Vólderín's inherent knowledge of the wild.

Léofric wondered how any living man could make it up those slopes clad in armor. The archers that Gollmorn had posted there must have been men used to the wild to be able to scale them, though how they came to be that way, living away from the wild in the cities, he could not tell.

Khrua left the night the Army made camp. Rothgaric called him before the royal tent to repay him. "You have done well. Any price you ask shall be given to you."

"Khrua want shiny weapon," Khrua-Hadrim said gruffly. "Shiny weapon much better than wooden club. With that, can kill traitor brother."

"You shall have the best that I can offer."

Rothgaric took a steel warhammer from the King's personal store and presented it to the Vólderín. Then the wild man left and disappeared into the mountains, Dunndag Greenmail and his men going with him. Léofric was not altogether sad to see the Vólderín go, for he thought him very strange. Yet there was something about his simple ways that evoked sympathy and compassion. Léofric wondered at this as he watched the Vólderín turn his hairy visage to the mountains and walk away from the camp into the golden light of the setting sun.

Two nights after the army set up camp within sight of some of the higher foothills, Léofric lay in his tent, unable to sleep due to an extreme, almost supernatural anxiety. He bit his nails in anticipation. His breath came in short quick gasps. He expected someone to enter at any moment.

He finally decided to seek refuge outside. Stepping outside into the warm late spring night, he lay down in a green place beneath the foothills. The night sky seemed to envelope him as he sank into a deep sleep.

Léofric saw the steep foothills rising before his clouded vision. He saw the cavalry of Irminsul spurring their horses up the steep slopes, making steady progress despite the hale of arrows that flew down upon them. The riders were protected by huge shields which they bore in front of them. They pressed up higher and higher. Their victory seemed sure, and Léofric became so excited that he ended the dream and awoke before it had a chance to completely finish.

He told himself that this was a small matter as he ran to report to his father. He had received the message. The particulars did not matter. He found Rothgaric and the captains holding their morning council in the royal tent.

"I have had another sword dream!"

Rothgaric looked up from the map slightly startled. "Well," he said seriously, "we have learned well the value of listening to you. What did you see?"

"The enemy archers are stationed atop the foothills. We must send cavalry up the slopes, protected with large shields to fend off the enemy's arrows. The archers will have nowhere to go, and must then either surrender or be killed. Gollmorn will then have precious few archers left."

Rothgaric's eyes brightened with pride. "Yes," he agreed, "Yes, you are right." Turning to the captains, he said, "Issue the order for the cavalry to attack immediately."

The horses were saddled and a force of two hundred cavalry rode to the foothills. The morning sun shone brightly on the bosses of their shields. Rebel archers, standing toe to toe, appeared on the edge of the summit and began loosing their shafts. It seemed as if the sun itself was blocked by the cloud of their arrows. Though these shafts were loosed repeatedly, they did no damage, but flew into the large shields borne by the cavalry of Irminsul with dull thuds.

"It is working, my boy," cried Rothgaric, clapping his son on the back as he watched from a crude watchtower constructed from some of the sparse trees that dotted the foothills.

The vanguard was about to reach the summit, when suddenly disaster struck. The lead horse lost his footing and tripped, causing a chain reaction down the line and horses and riders fell to the ground, many of them trapped under their fallen steeds, others too taken aback to save themselves.

This solicited a mighty cheer of victory from the archers on the summit. With renewed vigor, they immediately began pouring shaft upon shaft down on their fallen foes. Not one man escaped the deadly downpour, for those who endeavored to struggle from beneath their horses and massive shields quickly received shafts through their necks and chests. Maelthaen covered his ears in anguish and disgust, and endeavored to deaden the noise of the cheering rebel archers as he stormed back to his tent.

Rothgaric turned away in bewilderment. "How? Oh, how could this happen? You saw everything in your dream, did you not, Léofric? Everything was proceeding perfectly. Poor brave warriors.

Alas I could not save you. You shall not be forgotten. Not forgotten, but avenged."

"Léofric, truly I wish that the shafts that pierced the hearts of the valiant fallen soldiers would have found their mark in my breast. It was not their destiny to die this day."

Léofric turned away from his father. He could not face him now. He knew that it was because of his impetuousness that those brave men had died. If only he had let the sword dream run its course then they would have had victory! Now there was only more blood on his hands!

Léofric went back to his tent and wrestled with his heart for many hours. He longed for his mother's comforting embrace in this dark hour. Finally, he could bear it no longer, and went to find his father.

He found him discussing the next logical plan of action with his captains in the royal tent.

"My lord," Léofric said urgently, "I must speak with you now."

"Very well," he said. Turning back to his captains, he said, "leave us."

When the mail-clad men had left, Léofric fell down at his father's feet. "Father, forgive me, for I have once again been the instrument of our defeat. True, I told you what I saw in my dream, but in my excitement I cut the dream off before it was ended. If I had stayed asleep, I know I would have seen the manner in which to achieve victory. Forgive me, I beg you."

Rothgaric raised his son to his feet and embraced him. "Do not grieve so, my son. I wish you were not so impetuous, but you inherited that trait from me. I cannot find fault in you without finding the same fault in myself. Hone your skills and concentrate and you shall soon bring us victory."

Léofric bid his father goodnight and then went to bed, his burden somewhat lightened by his father's words, but still bearing heavy upon his soul.

ELEVEN

THE NIGHT ATTACK

One night, about a fortnight after the fall of the cavalry, Léofric went to his tent after supper to prepare for bed. He doffed his hauberk and hung it on the stand near the bed. Then he removed his boots and set them near the foot of the bed. He, like most of the men in the camp, slept almost fully dressed.

Léofric lay tossing and turning in his bed, wondering how the other men in the camp could sleep when they were surrounded by all the noises of the night. What was actually the quiet chirping of the crickets sounded like giants sawing wood to his mind. He thought he heard the howling of wolves in the wind, though he knew they were far from Firbolg Forest. The full moon seemed to glare directly through the large circular smoke opening above his head, making sleep impossible.

Léofric decided once again to seek refuge out under the stars. Wrapping a light cloak about him, he left the tent and walked out under the starry sky. It seemed that he could almost see his mother's face looking back at him in the moon, and he could feel a deep longing inside himself, a longing to see her and pour out all the feelings in his guilt-ridden heart to her. Forcing his mind to not think of such things, he closed his eyes and willed his feelings back down again.

The last thing he saw as he closed his eyes was the full moon shining down on his face. Slowly, his mind began to float absently in the darkness, in the mists of a separate reality. His subconscious wandered freely in the realm of dreams.

He saw the moon shining down lightly golden in his mind. As he watched a strange thing happened. The moon split and became two brightly burning fires. He saw that in an instant that these fires were spreading over the camp of the Army of Irminsul and saw riders in blackened mail with torches, burning and pillaging as they came. He could feel the incredible heat of the flames, and the nauseous billowing smoke filled his nostrils. The flames grew higher and higher and closed in around him. They seemed to be almost scorching his skin when suddenly he cried out and his eyes flew open. He was lying alone in the grass in the tranquil night and the camp was as it had been. He knew for certain that it was a sword dream, and that he had seen it all. This was the perfect chance to bring his father victory and make him proud. He immediately ran to find Rothgaric.

It was late at night, and the guards in front of the royal tent were all asleep, though it was their charge to remain awake throughout the night to protect the King. They lay there, eyes shut tightly, hands still clutching the shafts of their halberds. Flying into the royal tent unannounced, he ran to his father's bed and shook him awake. "Father, Father! You must awake. It is urgent."

"Wh-wh-what?" muttered Rothgaric groggily, rubbing his eyes and sitting up in bed.

"Father, listen! I have had a sword dream and this time I was careful to see it through to the end. Gollmorn is going to send raiders to burn and pillage the camp. He means to smoke us out. We must be ready to counter the attack."

"You are absolutely sure of this?" asked Rothgaric intently, though the look in his eyes was still somewhat dazed.

Léofric nodded. "Yes. I saw our camp burning quickly, the flames reaching higher and higher. We must act now, or our enemy will succeed. You must believe me."

"I do, son. Well done, my boy," cried Rothgaric, by this time fully awake. Léofric was thankful that his father had refused to lose faith in him, despite his past failures. He reflected that the grace his father showed to him was, after a fashion, akin to the Grace that The King That Is extended to all His children, regardless of their past deeds or failures.

Rothgaric took a battle horn from where it hung on a peg above the bedpost and blew three short blasts upon it. This was the sacred silver horn of the King of Irminsul, passed down for centuries from each King to his successor, which was only sounded when the need was dire. The unicorn of Irminsul was beautifully embossed near the mouth piece. It was said to be of Elven make, wrought at the command of Nilmeron, the Elven Lord whose union with Luaria of Irminsul began the line of half-Elven Kings.

Once he had blown it, the red man said, "The last time this horn was blown was the night the Sword Dreamer Helgi was discovered dead, murdered by the hand of Gollmorn. The elderly Sword Dreamer had dreamt of Gollmorn's treachery, but because of Helgi's old age, he could not alert Futhark before Gollmorn was upon him. Now the silver horn of Nilmeron sounds again, this time not to announce a tragedy, but to prevent one.

The camp was soon alive with activity. No torches were lit, as that would inform the enemy of their foreknowledge. A force of a hundred cavalry, under the command of Rothgaric himself, drew up a line before the camp and waited. For hours on end, no one was sighted. The men became anxious, itching for action, heels tingling to spur their mounts. Some even began to doubt the report of the Sword Dreamer. The horses fared no better, for they snorted and pawed the ground excitedly, sensing the tense feeling in the air.

Then, at about three o'clock in the morning, the lights of a dozen torches were seen bobbing up and down in the darkness, drawing nearer and nearer to camp.

"The enemy riders approach," hissed Rothgaric. "These are the raiders whom the Sword Dreamer has seen in his sword dream. Do not spur your mounts until they are so near that you can see the torch light gleam on their mail."

The enemy riders drew up before the assembled horsemen. It was so dark that even with their torches, the enemy did not see the large body of cavalry until they were only a few yards from them.

Upon seeing a hundred men, fully armed and waiting for them, the raiders successfully attempted to turn their horses and galloped back in the direction they had come.

"After them!" Rothgaric commanded. "In their confusion they will lead us back to their camp. Now, with the element of surprise on our side, we can rout the entire company."

They followed for several leagues at a safe distance, being careful not to lose sight of the fleeing riders. Finally they saw what appeared to be a camp in the darkness. Coming up closer on the heels of the pursued, they saw the falcon standard of the army of Gollmorn flying above the tents not far off.

They charged in, uttering cries of "Irminsul!" at the top of their lungs. They appeared suddenly, spurring their horses to the utmost exertion. The thundering of hooves was as an earthquake or an avalanche. The torch light reflected on their gleaming mail, suggesting the look of holy warriors come to deal out righteous judgment. The men in the camp did not know what to think when they beheld the shining host.

Fortunately, the camp was mostly deserted. The cries of the pursued added to the needed pandemonium. Groggy soldiers emerged half-armored from their tents and they were quickly put to the sword by the King's horsemen as they galloped past.

After the last man had been killed, the cavalry set to work looting. Little was found, other than the usual blackened steel armor and weapons of the enemy. Rothgaric was overseeing the looting of the tents, to see that no unnecessary violence erupted, when one of the soldiers caught him by the arm.

"My lord, I have found something that you should see."

He led him to a central tent that was the largest in the whole camp. Ducking inside, Rothgaric saw that it was filled with countless bags of grain, salted pork, and other food. It was enough food to sustain a massive army for a six-month siege. This apparently was what Gollmorn eventually intended to do.

Laughing, Rothgaric said, "This must be the enemy's entire food supply. So this is Gollmorn's supply camp. The regiments must come here from time to time to receive their rations. It is fortunate for us that he could not spare very many men to guard it. Burn it. He cannot survive long without it. Take nothing. We have more than enough supplies already."

The command quickly rang out through, the camp, "Burn the supply tent, by order of the King!"

All brush and debris were cleared away from around the supply tent, to keep the flames from reaching the tall flammable grass and starting a fire on the plain. The tent was then fired and soon became a pillar of roaring flames. The soldiers of Irminsul cheered and brandished their weapons as they watched the flaming tent shoot golden stalks of light into the starry night sky. The cavalry then mounted happily and rode back to camp, singing the victory songs of Irminsul to the joyous beat of their horses' hooves. When they returned with the news of the victory, the Army was overjoyed and celebrated the first great victory of the Sword Dreamer with many songs and much laughter. Léofric had finally brought his father victory. He was honored by a song that Maelthaen, having studied verse in his youth, had composed for him.

> *Hail, Oh hail to the Sword Dreamer!*
> *May he have long life and be well!*
> *Hail, oh hail to the Sword Dreamer!*
> *Let us raise our tankards of ale!*
> *Hail also to Rothgaric!*
> *To fight for him we have sworn!*
> *Hail, oh, hail to them both!*
> *We shall defeat Gollmorn!*

Léofric quietly took his leave before the festivities were over. As he walked back to his tent, the crunch of the grass beneath his feet reminded him of the triumphant galloping of the horses of Irminsul and his heart was glad.

As he lay in bed, looking up at the late night stars through the smoke hole of his tent, he said, "Gildéador, Lord of the Seven Stars, though my people know You not, I thank You for giving us the victory. If ever I am King, I will rule with Your Will foremost in my mind. Your Name shall be spoken with honor by men once again."

As Léofric was falling asleep, he glanced at his wolfskin cloak. The face of the wolf seemed somehow changed. A look of purpose and dignity was in its eyes.

TWELVE

A MESSAGE FROM THE ELVENLANDS

Although the celebration lasted into the early hours of the morning, with much feasting and drinking of ale, Léofric rose early the next morning, having slept like a lamb due to his encouraging success. Unlike the other men lounging about the camp, he did not have the after effects of too much ale pounding mercilessly at his skull, for he had wisely drunk only one tankard, when Maelthaen had finished his short but noteworthy song and they had all raised their tankards high. Maelthaen and some of the other commanders had endeavored to have him drink many different toasts throughout the night, but he had merely poured the contents of his pint on the ground when the slightly tipsy, overly merry captains were looking in the other direction. Before going to bed, as the feast fires were smoldering, and did little against the awakening pinkish blue sky, he spoke to his father of the temperance he had decided to show, and

Rothgaric told him he was proud. The red-bearded giant did not approve of heavy drinking.

"I am proud of you, my son. Even a good king or prince may endanger his position or his realm if he is under the influence of strong drink. You showed good judgment in practicing self control this night. Let no thing become your master, save a pure spirit and a sound mind."

As Léofric walked to the food supply tent, he heard a strange sound, like the clarion call of a trumpet. It sounded vaguely like the whinnying of a great warhorse. Yet it seemed to be coming from the sky. There came with it a great swooshing sound, as of massive wings rhythmically beating the air. The sound grew louder and louder, until a great wind rustled the surrounding tents.

Léofric looked up into the golden morning light and scanned the heavens wonderingly for a moment, and finally saw something that he had never dreamed he would ever live to see. A winged unicorn, like the one on the standards of the King, was flying down out of the sky, its hooves pawing the air as it came. Its coat was the color of the purest alabaster. Its legs were swift and strong. It had flown all the way from the Elvenlands, as unicorns only descended to that region from the heavens, yet it was not winded and seemed fresh. Léofric stared at it in disbelief. Several of the other men who had slept outside their tents, due to the failure to reach their beds the previous evening, stared in stupefied curiosity at the majestic sight, dumbfounded at what they saw.

The rider was even fairer to look upon than the mount. He was an Elven commander. His figure was incredibly tall and majestic. His locks were as red as rubies and as long as bonfire flames, and his green eyes sparkled like emeralds. He was clad in a gleaming hauberk, over which he wore a white surcoat. The surcoat was emblazoned with a large rectangular golden shield with an emerald as its boss. It was the treasured shield of Frékanéor and the standard of Nilmeronel. The elf's hands were protected by cloth-of-silver gauntlets. On his head, he wore a visorless sallet, a backsloping steel cap, under which his fiery locks flowed freely. This sallet was unusual for its kind, for it had large cheek plates at the chin straps. An ornate wing smelted over with silver rose from either side of the head. A finely crafted, single-handed broadsword with shiny bronze fittings and a grip wrapped in blue leather hung at his side. Every piece of his armament contributed to his inherent air of valor. Dumbstruck, Léofric's eyes widened in awe at the majestic sight.

Surgessar ran to meet the other elf, and saluted him as his unicorn landed. The dark elf had drunk only a little as well, for his race did not indulge much in drink, because they knew it clouded one's judgment.

"Elsté, Naemar!" Surgessar greeted the other Elven warrior.

"Elsté, Surgessar!" The Elven commander dismounted and returned the salute. Then he removed his helm, causing the sunlight to dance on the silvered wings, and holding it under his arm, grasped the dark elf's forearm tightly in his other hand. It had been several years since they had seen each other. They were brothers by oath of blood and the sword.

"I must speak with the King of Irminsul immediately."

"Come with me." The two elves began walking briskly toward the royal tent.

Léofric, having never seen a unicorn, or so mighty an elf, wanted to know more of the commander. He followed them at a safe distance, feeling too timid to make the acquaintance of so mighty an elf and reached the royal tent shortly after Surgessar and his companion. He ducked inside the royal tent and his father and Surgessar greeted him cheerfully. He found the King alone, for the captains were still greatly pleased with the victory of the previous night and did not wish to discuss further plans, and some were still sleeping off the ale.

When Léofric arrived, Surgessar and the Elven commander had only just entered. The fire-haired elf saluted Rothgaric. "Hail, Rothgaric of Irminsul! I am Naemar, general of the forces of the principality of Nilmeronel, and I come with a message from my master, Éalrohil, golden lord of Nilmeronel. He sends his greetings."

"Will he send aid for the sake of the old alliance of Nilmeron?" Rothgaric's face brightened with hope. This could give him a great advantage over the enemy. Ever since the ascension of Nilmeron to the throne of Irminsul, there had been an unwritten alliance between Irminsul and the Elven principality of Nilmeronel.

"Alas, no. He cannot help you, for our land is still recovering from the great plague that swept through the realm in winter. What is more, the Army is starving due to a poor harvest last autumn. The friendship of the King of Irminsul is very dear to his heart, but my lord says he cannot risk the lives of his people given these grave circumstances. But he sends his blessings, and his assurance that once this upstart Gollmorn is defeated, as he has full faith that he will be, there shall be a renewed friendship between his realm and yours." Naemar saluted again and turned to go.

"I was counting on your aid, friend," Surgessar said sadly, his eyes becoming shrouded with the dismay that only comes from being refused by a brother.

Naemar turned at the flap of the tent, looking sadly back at Surgessar. It pained him greatly to be the bearer of such sad tidings, all the more because Surgessar was like a brother to him. The two elves had been taught to fight by Surgessar's father Almiras, the greatest swordsman the Elvenlands had ever produced. He felt now as if he were plunging his blade deep into his friend's breast, and it tortured his own heart to refuse him help.

"If it were my decision, brother," Naemar said earnestly, "I would send the largest force I could muster. But it is my master's decision, not mine. The only aid I can give you is this: remember your friends to the sky."

Naemar left, and in a moment, those in the tent of the King heard a mighty neighing as his winged steed galloped up into the sky amidst the beating of its great wings. Surgessar shook his head. They could expect no aid from Nilmeronel.

THIRTEEN

AN UNLIKELY VISITOR

That evening, long after General Naemar of Nilmeronel had left, there came another unlikely warrior to the camp of the Army of Irminsul on foot from the south. As Léofric was walking toward the southern end of the camp, he heard an irritated voice in fast conversation with the sentries. He could not hear what they were saying, but soon saw the sentries leading a finely armored warrior toward the royal tent. He was extremely short, standing just over four feet tall, but of extremely powerful build. He had a long, bushy flaxen beard with many fair, braided strands. His long yellow mane was hidden by a great round helmet with a slight mail skirting. The helmet also had rims around the eyes for protection. Both the helmet, and the mail skirting were smelted over with silver, making the helm shine in the moonlight as he walked under the stars. He wore a small hauberk of blue steel mail that was of the best workmanship Léofric had ever seen, even in the camp of Irminsul. His offensive armor included two bearded axes with stout shafts of ash wood. The heads were finely tempered and beautiful. Upon one was etched the knot-worked head of a dragon. Upon the other was etched the head of a snow troll with its large fangs bared.

Léofric knew him immediately to be a dwarf, such as were mentioned in a few obscure children's tales in villages near the southern end of the Southlands. They were said to be a strange folk living somewhere south of southern Kjartens. Léofric had never dreamed he would ever live to see a creature he had thought only to exist in folk tales.

As the dwarf passed by the forges of the weapon smiths, he accidentally brushed against Kettil, and looked at him curiously, as if he had seen the old smith's face somewhere before.

"I am looking for the man in charge," he said authoritatively. His voice was deep and somewhat gravelly. Léofric followed at a distance as the Dwarven warrior was led to the royal tent.

"I am Cynric, son of Cýling, the most fearsome fighter in all the Dwarvenlands. I desire to fight for you."

Rothgaric smiled, amused. "But why, master dwarf? Is there not enough fighting in your land with the snow trolls and malevolent dragons?"

"I have just come from killing Framgar the snow troll, at last freeing my people from his cruel dominion. My life is complete, and I would die fighting in battle, as death in the heat of battle is the greatest honor among my people."

Rothgaric smiled broadly. "But we will be fighting tall men and cavalry. I doubt not your heart. But for you to fight for us...." He began rumbling with laughter.

Cynric became hot with anger. He stalked over to Roth-garic, and, before the guards could react, seized him violently by the foot and tossed him high into the air. The red-bearded man came crashing down on his back, upsetting the table on which the map of Irminsul lay.

Looking up, astonished and somewhat shaken, he exclaimed, "I have heard of the immense strength of your race, but I never thought a small dwarf could toss a full-grown man in full mail. You shall fight for us. We could definitely use a warrior of your quality." Cynric smiled and left the royal tent.

Later, Léofric said to Surgessar, "I did not think I would ever live see a dwarf. Tell me what you know of them."

Surgessar smiled, "First, a small lesson in geography. You know that to the north of the northern Kjartens lie the Elvenlands. And to the south, rimmed by the Kjartens, lies Irminsul, the land of men. To the east of the eastern Kjartens and the west of the western Kjartens is the Elverean Sea." The two friends began walking in the direction of Léofric's tent.

"But south of the southern Kjartens is the Dwarvenlands. It is a harsh land of snow and ice, populated by dragons and trolls. The dwarves live very hard lives, for they are always hard-pressed by the malevolent dragons and trolls. They live for war, thus they are the best weapon smiths the world. For them death in battle is the great-est glory. They never journey north of the mountains. The elves call the whole continent, including the Dwarvenlands, Éalindé, 'the land that is', for it was made in its original beauty by Gildéador, before the Dark Enemy came to sow discord. The southern land that is now the Dwarvenlands was once fertile and green.

"But the Dark Enemy invaded and took it for his own, setting up his base of power there and turning the good green land into a wasteland of ice and snow. The Dark Enemy also made evil minions for himself out of the cold stone. These vile creature were short in stature with beards like iron wire. His evil fire burned red in their eyes and their skin was the hue of greenish muck. They were called by my people the Duavrin, the dark little terrors. They began to spread northward, reaching the base of the Southern Kjartens, and even up in their safe, beautiful northern homeland, my people felt threatened.

"Gildéador spoke to the mind of a master Elven healer and swordsmith named Aelgaelfyn, whose name means "fire heart" in the ancient Elvish tongue, to journey to the land of ice and snow and eliminate the threat of the Dark Enemy's minions there. A great battle was fought near the base of the Southern Kjartens, Aelgaelfyn, fought single-handedly against evil dragons, trolls and Duavrin. He swung his sword in great strokes, singing to Gildéador with all his might. As the sun rose on the fifth day, Aelgaelfyn saw that all his foes lay dead about him. While searching among the dead, Aelgaelfyn saw that five of the Duarvrin still lived. Gildéador gave him the inspiration and the ability to exorcise the evil from these creatures, and they became the five patriarchs of the dwarves, the adopted children of Gildéador. Gildéador then created mates for these fathers of the dwarves, and their children spread throughout the icy wastelands, driving out the last of the Duavrin with the weapons they made from the knowledge birthed by Gildéador through Aelgaelfyn in their cleansed minds.

"The Dark Enemy then fled underground for a time, having suffered a defeat at his very base of power. He was seen in that land no more, though it remains an icy wasteland to this day and many malevolent dragons and trolls still dwell there. The work of the Dwarven smiths exceeds even the best steelcraft of the fire elves of Aelgaelisel. You saw the dwarf's armor. Though the fire elves can make blued sword blades, only the smiths of the Dwarvenlands know how to work the fire in just such a way as to make blued mail. It is a hallowed secret that is kept safe among them. It has something to do with the heat of the forge fire, for the incredible heat produced by the fire mountains in the Elven Kingdom of Aelgaelisel is nothing compared to that produced by the fire mountains of the Dwarvenlands. The mountains of the Dwarvenlands in ancient days spewed forth the anger and malice of the Dark Enemy. Now the adopted children of Gildéador use them in their fight to drive away all the minions of the Dark Enemy that still remain in their icy homeland. The fire mountains of the Dwarvenlands serve as a good lesson to us: what the forces of evil intend to use for evil, The King That Is ultimately uses for the good of His servants."

Léofric sat down on the ground and drew his knees up to his chest. The stars of early evening gazed down upon them.

Looking up at the dark elf, the young man asked, "How do you know so much of the dwarves, Surgessar? They live so far from your homeland."

"Years ago, when I was young and Éalrohil of Nilmeronel was just a princeling, a curse was put upon his sister, the princess Galithwyn, by a servant of the Dark Enemy. The only thing that could save her was a flower deep under the ice of the Dwarvenlands. Éalrohil's father, Galifas, sent me to the Dwarvenlands to retrieve it. During my long search, I dwelt for a time in the longhouse of Cynric's grandfather, Ingric. The dwarves are suspicious of strangers, no elf having journeyed there since the days of Aelgaelfyn, but Ingric and his clan befriended me once I proved myself with the blade. When my search proved successful, I returned to Nilmeronel. I had made a crossbow for young Cýling, for which favor he promised to fight in battle alongside me someday. His son will now fulfill that promise. Cýling prized that weapon, as the dwarves do not know how to make crossbows."

"Please," said Léofric, "Tell me more of Aelgaelfyn and his long single-handed battle against the forces of the Dark Enemy in the Dwarvenlands. I am anxious to hear it, for I did not hear such tales growing up in the Southlands"

"Ah," the dark elf said merrily, his eyes brightening, "but, you see, he did not fight them all alone. He had his brave mount, the first unicorn to come down to Éalindé. He was the first mairnéor, or unicorn rider. Look up in the heavens. Occasionally you will see a star, traveling rapidly across the night sky. These are the cavalrymen of the personal Army of The King That Is. They do battle against the forces of the Dark Enemy in the heavens. Every thousand years a star will fall to the earth. This star is a unicorn, and the Elven warrior destined by Gildéador to be its rider will find it and it shall submit to him. My blood brother Naemar was just such a warrior. You saw his beautiful winged beast. Aelgaelfyn was the first Elven warrior to receive a unicorn. In truth, he looked very much like Naemar, with long fiery hair and emerald eyes that blazed with his love of Gildéador.

"After him, there was Nilmeron of Gladdéas, who rode his great winged horse down into Irminsul to serve as a mercenary. After he became King, the standard of the Army of Irminsul bore a white unicorn, and that has been the symbol of the nation since the day of Nilmeron's coronation. When a unicorn rider falls in battle, his spirit is taken up into the night sky, to fight against the forces of the Dark Enemy in the heavens.

"But Aelgaelfyn, the first unicorn rider, was the greatest weapon smith of the Elvenlands in his age. When Gildéador called him to rid the icy southern lands of Éalindé of the servants of the Dark Enemy, he made in his smithy the greatest armaments ever forged up to that time, and armed with these masterpieces of smith-craft he flew on his great winged steed to the south. He was clad in a long shirt of whitened steel mail that reached past his knees. On his head, he wore a finely crafted, nasaled barbute that was smelted over with white gold. His long sword hung in a baldric and scabbard of golden silk on his back. Aelgaelfyn was tall, almost half a foot taller than I, standing at two inches above seven feet. As you can imagine, the blade itself was about five and a half feet long, and it was of strong whitened steel. The fittings were of pure gold. The pommel was lobed and both it and the short guard were etched with swirling designs and Elvish words, prayers to The King That Is for protection and strength in battle. The double-handed grip was wrapped in rich brown leather. He had named the great weapon Cludamair, 'Unicorn Blade'.

"He had also made spiked greaves smelted over with white gold, which he put on the legs of his flying mount. As he came to the place where the forces of the dark enemy were mustering, he lifted his great sword high above his head. The blade flashed brilliantly, even though dark clouds obscured the sun. Diving down out of the sky with a great cry, he swung his great sword in a mighty downward stroke and hewed off the head of a massive troll warrior. Thus, the battle began. In the fray, the great unicorn of Aelgaelfyn slew as many enemies with his sharp horn and spiked greaves as did his master with his great sword. After the battle and the cleansing of the five remaining Duavrin, Aelgaelfyn forged swords for the new children of Gildéador, and these were greatly treasured by them and passed down from one generation to the next. He also taught them the craft of weapon forging, in which they soon surpassed even him."

"That was a truly inspiring tale. But why do we never see any dwarves here in Irminsul?"

"No dwarves ever journey north of the southern Kjartens. None before Cynric Cýling's son, that is."

"At least one did before him." Léofric and Surgessar turned to see Kettil the weapon smith standing nearby. Apparently, the short smith had been standing next to Léofric's tent, listening to the dark elf's tale for some time, unnoticed.

"My father, Fréawulf Frost Hammer, one of the best of the Dwarven smiths, journeyed north into the Southlands of Irminsul to seek adventure. Instead of battle, he found and married a beautiful country maiden, the fair Elanéath, my mother. I have his Dwarven blood flowing in my veins. It is from my father that I get my great strength. I am honored to have taken up his trade at his behest. I admit, humbly, that I am somewhat skilled in my craft, but I can make nothing to match his masterpieces."

Léofric strode to his tent, yawning and stretching his arms above his head. He lay for a long time on his cot, looking absent-mindedly into the eyes of the wolf's head and pondering all that he had seen and heard that day. He hoped to know more of this Dwarven warrior, Cynric Cýling's son, slayer of Framgar the great snow troll. He also desired to know more of the tale of Kettil the half-Dwarven smith of the Army of Irminsul.

FOURTEEN

A DWARVEN RITUAL

The next evening, rations were increased to ensure that the men would be well-fed before the next battle. The battle would be soon in coming, for it was certain that the enemy would not tarry long in striking back in retribution for the burning of his supplies.

That night, many fires were lit, and the men gathered around with bowls of stew, chunks of bread and tankards of ale. Cynric was there also, and he sat with a group of slightly older soldiers and he was recounting some of the tales of his many adventures. Were it not for his beard and muscular figure, it would have been thought that a child had donned armor and run from his home and mother to fight with the Army.

Out of curiosity, Léofric kept a close watch on him. Truly, the short warrior's appetite was greater than that of a full-grown man. Altogether, he had downed eight bowls of stew and quaffed fifteen tankards of ale, yet he was in no way tipsy or sick to the stomach. The bearded axeman's table manners were not in the least refined, but for all that, Léofric found him to be the jolliest warrior he had met, since he had lost his dear friend Halifar in his first sword dreaming battle. The dwarf talked and laughed loudly, occasionally breaking into a lay or shorter song recounting the deeds of the five fathers of the dwarves, or other highly honored warriors or weapon smiths.

Kettil approached the dwarf, pumped his hand, and spoke to him softly for a moment. Cynric's eyes brightened and he exclaimed, "So this is the son of Fréawulf the wanderer. After he passed over the southern Kjartens into Irminsul, my people knew nothing of him. He was the greatest smith of his age, and one of the greatest warriors. He has now become a popular legend in his homeland. A large likeness of his face is now carved into the side of the fire mountain of Hjarbried, where he set up his forge. I see his face in yours. That is why I looked at you strangely when I arrived. I am proud to have made the acquaintance the son of Fréawulf Frost Hammer before I go someday to dwell at last in the halls of my ancestors. My friend, if you have half the skill with a hammer and anvil as your father did, you shall be the most renowned smith in all of Irminsul, to be sure."

Kettil laughed and then began to sing a short song that he himself had composed:

"Blades of Aelgaelisel,
Ring mail of the Dwarvenlands,
I pray thee, pray thee
Come and see
The work of these unworthy hands.

Even though my work is poor,
And I am but an ignorant boar,
Yet, a work of my hand
May one day prove worthy of lore."

Cynric clapped his hands and laughed aloud. "Well sung, master smith."

The blond-bearded dwarf then noticed the young man watching him and grinned broadly. "You are the red-bearded man's son, Léofric was it? My lad, you have the look of a fighter in your eyes. You may fight in your first battle soon, shall you not?"

Léofric asserted that he hoped he would, even though he knew his father was very protective of the Sword Dreamer.

Cynric chuckled to himself. "I remember my first battle." He leaned forward excitedly and asked, "Are you at all frightened?"

Léofric leaned forward and whispered that he was. The dwarf winked. "I know the perfect remedy for that: the Reel of the Ice Sword. It is the way the warriors of the Dwarvenlands gain courage for battle. Perhaps I could demonstrate. Let me see. If only we had some music…Ah!"

He had had been scanning the surrounding crowd with his eyes as he spoke, and had noticed, out of the corner of his eye, that one of the pages was carrying a lute. Walking over to the young man he said, "I say, boy, can you play that?"

"As well as any minstrel of Auraheim, master dwarf," the boy retorted, a slightly perturbed look in his eye. He prided himself on his ability to play, and felt that the dwarf's question was presumptuous.

"Very good," Cynric said, smiling. "Now, would you be so good as to play what I show you?"

The dwarf seized the instrument from the page and began plucking the strings madly. The music sounded like some insane jig danced by the drunken ruffians in the various inns of the Southlands. Cynric Cýling's son handed the lute back to the page who tried to the best of his ability to follow the dwarf's lead.

"Mirror me, laddie. You will need your sword. I shall only use one of my axes. By the by, did I tell you that the heads of my axes were forged from the shards of the sword Skofnung, one of the five swords that were forged by the Elven mage, healer and smith Aelgaelfyn? He made them for the five original chieftains of the dwarves whom he changed from Duarvrin. Skofnung was an heirloom of my house, and after my father died and it broke in battle, the shards passed to me and I had them forged into new weapons, weapons of blessed steel with which I could kill Framgar the snow troll. The steel of that sacred sword is now in the heads of these good battle axes I bear."

The beginning of the dance involved running forward toward the partner and back, always facing him, gently yet quickly swinging one's weapons at each other in mock battle when one came near the other. This step was in a way almost frightening to Léofric, as he thought on several occasions that the dwarf would accidentally run too close and split open his skull with his Dwarven axe.

In the next step, Cynric and Léofric locked mailed arm in mailed arm and swung around in a circle. Finally they placed the empty hand on the corresponding hip and held the hand holding the weapon high above their heads, dancing around in a circle on one foot. The steps were then repeated. The other soldiers soon noticed the wild display and began laughing and clapping in time with the music.

The tempo of the music became faster and faster and with it so did the repetition of the steps. Léofric felt his face burn with exertion. As the speed of the dance increased, he lost sense of his surroundings. As the reel reached its height, he was only conscious of himself, the dwarf and the dance. His apprehension melted away and a fiery courage filled his heart. He was filled with an almost supernatural confidence, and he no longer doubted himself or his ability as a fighter.

Then, just as it seemed that the dance could not become any faster, Cynric bellowed, "Stop." Léofric and the dwarf fell instantly to the ground, and lay there motionless, their chests heaving. Léofric could feel his mind and nerves inwardly rejoicing, though he was too weary and sore from the mad dancing to notice their vibrant tingling. After several moments, the lad had caught his breath and struggled to his feet.

Léofric suddenly realized that he was sweating profusely. He wiped his brow and smiled.

"It worked, did it not?" the dwarf asked, beaming. Mighty Cynric Cýling's son was born of so spry a race that he had leapt to his feet long before Léofric could struggle to a standing position. The boy silently marveled at the dwarf's great endurance.

Léofric nodded and laughed, gulping in the precious air. Cynric Cýling's son boomed with laughter in return. This had been the first time that Léofric had ever danced, and he had done so in a Dwarven battle ritual. He had always been too timid to dance at any of the summer fairs at home in the Southlands. He fell asleep that night, his muscles sore, his heard still pounding like a marching drum, and the mad strumming still echoed in his ears. He was truly an astounding creature, this dwarf.

FIFTEEN

THE FINAL CONFRONTATION

The rebels' night raid on the camp of the Army of Irminsul had ended in disaster for the army of Gollmorn. The tables had been turned with the help of the Sword Dreamer. What Gollmorn had intended to do to Rothgaric, Rothgaric had done to him. Gollmorn had returned to find his supply tent a heap of cinders. He stood there for a moment, speechless with shock. Then his body began to tremble with anger. He took off one of the blackened mail gauntlets he wore and ground it into the grassy loam with his booted foot, putting as much of his seething, heathen anger as he could enter the furious stamping motion. Silently, he cursed Rothgaric with black oaths, reserving the darkest ones for his Sword Dreamer. This once inexperienced boy had become a formidable enemy, one that may cost him the war.

"He will lead us to our death now," one of Gollmorn's bodyguards whispered to a companion through clenched teeth. "Jarkin is by no means jovial, but he may prove a kinder master than the old whip slasher."

Gollmorn's keen ears pricked as he heard the guard's comment, and the rebel general turned and plunged his dagger into the unsuspecting man's breast. Then he turned back and walked swiftly to his tent, leaving the other guards standing in fear but not disbelief.

He sat there before his map in his tent for many hours. He sat in an ornate, carven chair, one of the spoils of victory of a battle at the beginning of the war, his mind racing with angry, fuming thoughts and schemes. All his supplies were destroyed, and, if what he had just overheard was any indication, his army was bordering on insurrection. He could not dispatch all of the malcontents, for, as much as he hated them, he needed them. As he sat alone in his tent, his mind boiling with anger and malice, he suddenly hit upon a bold stratagem. He would not surrender, as his men truly desired but never voiced for fear of his wrath. He had forsworn his soul to his mad, all-encompassing dream, and it would not release him, even if defeat were certain.

He would meet the Army of Irminsul in battle but half a league from Auraheim. He would trust in his strength of numbers to give him the victory. His infantry was over twice the size of Rothgaric's and his calvery was a man for man match. Once the Army of Irminsul was defeated, he would ride to the Silver City and the people, having no other alternative, would be forced to hail him as their king. It was a bold move, but it seemed his only route to success.

Khrua-Hadrim returned from the mountains to the camp of Irminsul very soon after the night raid. For some strange reason he had the intention to fight alongside the forces of Rothgaric in the coming battle. He had sewn deer bones into his cloak, turning it into a sort of primitive brigandine. The makeshift armor did not provide much protection, as it was just a cloak with bone fragments stitched helter-skelter across and down it, but it nevertheless gave him a look of savage majesty.

"But why do you help us now?" Léofric asked him at supper that night. "Why should you care who is victorious?"

"Traitor brother Khard-Ghurad fights with wicked hetman. Must kill him. Must avenge father."

After once again giving up the conversation, just as he had when first meeting Khrua-Hadrim, Léofric went to sit by the dwarf. His eyes lingered on the heads of the axes which hung in a double baldric on the dwarf's back. The etched images gave the weapons a noble appearance.

Seeing Léofric's gaze out of the corner of his eye, the dwarf drew them out and showed them to him. Indicating the dragon head, he said, "That was Fjolnir." Pointing to the troll, he said, "And that was Gurdag. I killed them both in my quest against Framgar's forces. Each ruled over his own fire mountain, but they were mice compared to Framgar himself.

"Framgar used intimidation to keep his minions from turning against him. He was a black-hearted genius, a genius for a troll, I mean. Framgar and his thugs terrorized my people for twelve years. It was during this time that my father died. On his deathbed, he made me swear that I would kill Framgar and save our people. I had many adventures in my quest against Framgar. If I survive tomorrow's battle, before I seek another, I will tell you of my many adventures."

"I will look forward to that, and shall enjoy listening to the many tales of your adventures in your snowbound homeland."

"Very well then," the blond dwarf said, laughing and slapping his knee.

Dunndag Greenmail and his men had returned with the Vólderín. When the Vuldervogund chieftain saw Cynric the dwarf, he exclaimed, "You are like short men from old Voldervogund tales. Voldervogund lore says short ancestors came north into mountains from icy southern home. Wanted to find better home. Traveled over ring of mountains, but could never get over. Bad weather. Many storms."

The dwarf merely raised his eyebrows at all that the mountain ranger had said.

Léofric walked about the camp for over an hour that night, observing the men in their preparation for the coming battle. The armorers cleaned the rust and impurities off of helmets, shields, hauberk and weapons, performing their duties ever under the watchful eye of Kettil. Léofric had an even deeper respect for the master weapon smith's handiwork now that he knew that Kettil had the blood of a dwarf master craftsman flowing in his veins.

Maelthaen was fitting a new saddle onto Beornost's back. The roan stallion's leg had mended quickly and he was ready for service. The flaxen-haired captain would ride his old charger into battle on the following day. Maelthaen had an understanding of his mount that was seldom found south of the Elvenlands.

Léofric walked among the fires, occasionally stopping to talk to men with whom he had become well-acquainted over the past months. These men were his brothers, his family, and he cared very much for them. Yet, if this truly was his family, he reflected, tomorrow it could stand on the edge of a knife, and all that he had come to hold dear, his father, Surgessar, even his love, Súndéa, could be gone by the time the sun sank in the west on the morrow. Silently, he prayed to The King That Is for protection and victory for himself and his friends.

All of Gollmorn's movements were reported by spies to Rothgaric on the morning of the third day after the night raid. This day, the armies would meet in what may be the final conflict of the war. Strangely, Léofric had not come to the royal tent that morning. Usually he arrived early, for, as the Sword Dreamer, he was a key part of the strategic planning. His father therefore went to go make inquiries.

Though he never spoke of it, Rothgaric enjoyed the fact that Léofric came to the royal tent every morning. It was, after a fashion, Rothgaric's manner of atoning for all the time lost when Léofric had been growing up.

"Maelthaen, have you seen the Sword Dreamer this morning?"

The golden-haired warrior shook his head. "I know not where he is, honestly. I would suppose he is still in his tent, for I have not seen him since supper last night."

When Rothgaric queried Surgessar, the dark elf replied in similar fashion and accompanied Rothgaric on his search.

Rothgaric and Surgessar found Léofric standing in his tent, madly rubbing his temples, his eyes closed tightly, as if in pain.

"What ails you, my son?" Rothgaric asked, his brow creased with worry.

"I do not know. I-I cannot think."

Surgessar nodded knowingly. "It is the after effects of a successful sword dream. It takes a few days to fully take effect. That is why neither of you noticed any difference. The Sword Dreamer's powers are useless after all the excitement of the victory."

Rothgaric sighed. "I do not know what to do in this case. I was counting on your aid before the battle."

Léofric's eyes opened suddenly and hardened with determination. "Father, I can fight."

"No, Léofric. You are too valuable to fight in battle. You are now skilled in the art of the blade, but even a skilled swordsman can be overwhelmed by greater numbers on the field of battle. No, I cannot risk the life of the Sword Dreamer."

"But my powers will be of no use to you today. You will need every sword you can get, skilled or unskilled. Please father, let me fight, I beg you."

Rothgaric drew in a deep breath and finally said, "Very well, my son. May my teaching serve you well this day. If we succeed, but I am killed, you shall be King. Rule honestly and justly and do not forget from whence you have come or Who it is who gives you your power." He laid a firm hand for a moment on Léofric's shoulder and the boy never forgot the feeling of confidence it sent through his whole being.

Rothgaric left his son to prepare for battle. Turning to Surgessar, he said, "Gollmorn will bring many infantry. I do not know how to deal with them. We have only cavalry, and the enemy of pikemen could make short work of us by aiming their long weapons at the mounts and unhorsing our riders. What can I do? "

Surgessar smiled and laid a hand on his friend's shoulder. "Leave that difficulty to me, my old friend. Naemar gave me the answer."

As the two warriors left, Léofric looked to see the head of the wolf pelt bathed in sunlight, the golden rays joining to form almost a crown, giving it a look of nobility and power. The wolf was now a king.

As Léofric mounted his horse, Kettil the half-Dwarven weapon smith suddenly came running. "Tarry, young master. I have a gift for you to use in battle." He unwrapped something small and round from a midnight blue cloth, and handed it up to Léofric. It was a small, finely wrought buckler. The central boss and rim were blued and the circle surrounding the boss was smelted over with shining silver. A double-bladed Dwarven battle axe was etched upon the boss.

"This is the shield Gramscylde. It belonged to my father, and I can think of no one more worthy to bear it into battle. My father was called Frost Hammer because his weapon of choice was a single-handed battle hammer with a great cubic head of Dwarven blue steel inlaid with bits of white gold. Its shaft was coated in silver. It was his finest piece of craftsmanship. He bore it along with this shield, which he also made. For him it was a great back shield, but it can easily fit the hand of a tall human youth such as you. May you be protected in battle today, lad. My prayers are with you."

It was a warm spring day, hinting a little of the coming summer, as the Army of Irminsul, in all its glory, rode out to the field of battle. The banners of silver emblazoned with the white unicorn fluttered in the light, warm breeze. Rothgaric rode first, for the first time wearing the silvered mail of the King. The sun sparkled on his armor. He wore a round silver helmet with a gold-plated nasal under which his fiery locks flowed freely. His forearms and wrists were protected by silvered vambraces embossed with unicorns. He still wore his old broadsword that he had born for years, for it reminded him of the humble background from which he had come. He rode the young white stallion of the King, a descendant of Maelros who still had an understanding of Elvish speech, an understanding that had passed through the pure blood line, even though his race long ago left their ancestral homeland north of the northern Kjartens.

Léofric rode behind. In addition to his hauberk, he wore a finely wrought coif of Elven make upon his head, a gift of Surgessar. Forged on near the top of the mail hood was a silver plated steel band, reaching all around the circumference of the head, for extra protection of the temples. The word Tengaelon, which was the Elvish term for "courage", was etched in Elvish runes along the length of the band. In his younger days, it had served the dark elf well in many a battle. He thought it a fitting gift for the High Prince, who would need protection for his head. It truly was piece of armor worthy of a prince, even Nilmeron himself.

Léofric and Surgessar had had their good friend Kettil etch five beautiful four-sided Elven stars on the blade of Léofric's light broadsword, under Surgessar's direction. Léofric was very pleased and named the sword Cluda Cluadrimarion: "Blade of the Stars". Armed with and defended by the best steel craft of all the free peoples of Éalindé, Léofric rode to battle, the first Sword Dreamer to ever bear sword against the enemies of Irminsul in battle.

As he rode, a song came to his mind, a beautiful song, and he sang it silently as a prayer, an entreaty to Gildéador for courage and protection in battle.

Oh, Gildéador hear my cry,
Gilda Éalindéarion.
Give courage to the Sword Dreamer, I,
Cludalathon Irminsularion.
I do not have a spirit of fear or shame,
Valuar Tengaelonarion.
But a sound mind so I can honor Your Name,
Gilda Valunanarion.

The song gave courage to Léofric's heart and he steeled himself for battle.

Súndéa wore her brigandine of purple cloth, along with a silver-plated conical helmet etched on the front with the convex four-sided star that for centuries had graced the silver scepter of the prince of Nilmeronel. Her beautiful helm also had a long mail skirting that was as delicate as the gossamer dresses of the maidens of Nilmeronel, yet almost as strong as the blued mail that Cynric the dwarf wore. It reached to the nape of the neck.

Surgessar wore his hauberk and plain blue surcoat, and a round helmet that was of blue steel. It was embossed with a small silver sun on the front and a small, cratered, full silver moon on the back. Reaching down to the neck were several strips of boiled leather, each six inches in length, dyed dark blue and sewn with several small strands of mail for extra protection for the neck. The elf's long dark mane flowed down far past these hanging straps.

Through the success of the night attack and the prospect of the end of the war, Rothgaric had been transformed. He was no longer Rothgaric the general, but Rothgaric the King, though he had not yet been crowned. He now wore his kingly armor unashamedly, and all could see the change it brought to his bearing, for now he bore himself as a ruler rather than just a leader of fighting men.

Behind him rode the dark elf and all his other captains, their surcoats reflecting the morning light. Riding behind Surgessar on his horse was Cynric, in his full Dwarven battle array. He was happy to fulfill the promise of his father. Behind the captains rode Léofric and Súndéa, leading the entire cavalry of Irminsul. The short Vuldervogund rangers begrudgingly rode behind a score of hand-selected men. All of them, especially Dunndag, were very much bothered, and did not enjoy the ride at all, as they were all very timid of horses, having never ridden them in their mountainous home.

The sun shone brightly on the armor of the horsemen and it seemed to Léofric that they had been made for this very battle. Yet, a shadow of sadness had settled over his countenance. Turning to the dark Elven girl, he said in a quiet voice, "My lady, I do not know if I shall live to see you again after the day is done."

She smiled warmly, "Do not worry, my dear warrior. Whatever happens, I am thankful that I have known you, and rest assured: even if you are gravely wounded or yes, even killed, I shall carry you in my heart forever, no matter what may happen on the battlefield today. I am glad to fight alongside the one I love." Léofric was greatly comforted by this and his thoughts then turned to the duty that lay ahead.

"I love you, and shall carry you in my heart always," he said earnestly, his voice and expression unwavering.

"In life," the dark Elven girl said sapiently, "loved ones come and go. Nothing lasts forever. Only Gildéador is eternal. When you lose a loved one, you must keep them with you in your heart. I never knew my mother, but I see her in my father. She is in my heart forever, for she beseeched the King That Is on my behalf as she gave birth to me, for she knew she would not live to see me grow to womanhood. I know that her love and wisdom are with me."

Léofric was amazed by her wisdom, and The King That Is gave him a deep, profound peace through her comforting words.

The two armies drew close upon the field of battle, the silver towers of Auraheim in the distance. On the left side of the plain was the gleaming silvery Army of Irminsul,, the banners of the white unicorn flapping in the morning breeze high above their heads. On the other side was the vile army of Gollmorn, clad in blackened mail, bearing the red falcon on the field of black, which Gollmorn had selected as the standard of his army. They stood there, a massive army of infantrymen and cavalrymen, all waiting for the villainous general's command. Their blackened halberds and spears pointed upward, bristling toward the sky, as if they were trying to slay the very sun. The men had long awaited action and were eager for battle. They could almost feel in their hands the spoils of victory.

Gollmorn sat before them on a black foaming stallion. He was a gaunt man, his black goatee meticulously combed to a sharp point. His green eyes were snakelike; their evil aura betrayed his mad vision. He did not care how many expendable men died, only that he achieve his all-encompassing ambition. He was clad in blackened mail and wore a black barbute with a steel horn on either side.

Even through the massive sound of the marching army and stallions, there was a silence that was so tangible, it could almost be cut with a knife. Hands in mail gauntlets became wet with perspiration, and beads of sweat dotted the hot foreheads of the soldiers beneath their open-faced helms. Cavalrymen and horses breathed heavily on both sides. A strange mixture of excitement and fear churned rapidly in the hearts of all present.

Suddenly, in the dead silence before the battle, the neighing of a great horse was heard overhead. All eyes turned skyward. To the amazement of all assembled, the flying unicorn of Naemar flew down in the golden morning light and alighted next to Surgessar. The general bore a long-shafted spear with the golden shield standard of Nilmeronel tied near the large, silver-plated head. The massive head was wrought in the shape of the horn of a unicorn. The white banner flapped proudly in the breeze.

The fiery-haired Elven general put a hand on his friend's shoulder. "Elsté! Today is a fine day for a battle."

The dark elf stared in disbelief. "It was my belief that your lord would not aid us."

The green-eyed elf laughed. "And so he will not. I am here of my own accord. My master has permitted it. My noble steed Ilondemair and I shall aid you this day."

Surgessar smiled proudly. "You are a true warrior and friend, my blood brother. Faethas!"

Rothgaric's eyes widened with hatred as he saw the rebel leader. Turning to his men, he shouted, "In the past you have died for Futhark. Now I ask you to die for me. But do not do it as you would for your King. Do it as you would for a brother. For are you not my brothers? You have bled with me and shared both in my tears and in my joy. You are my brothers, be you man or elf. I am also honored that a dwarf fights alongside me: representatives of each of the free races of Éalindé, standing together, united in the fight against one whose mind has been corrupted by the Dark Enemy, who gives birth to and controls all things that are evil.

"A grave shadow looms over our home. You may not want to fight this day, but what shall you tell your mothers, your fathers, your children, when they suffer under the yolk of a madman? Shall you tell them, as they are being whipped and downtrodden with toil, that you would not stand your ground? Or shall you tell them the day you return triumphant to them that you stood and fought for their freedom and the freedom of those not yet born? How do you answer? Will you stand with me?"

There was a great cry of, "Hail Rothgaric, King!" Then the men brandished their weapons on high.

At this, Surgessar ran to the center of the field, knelt to the ground, and began hurriedly making markings in the dirt with his dagger and mumbling in Elvish. The dagger was single-edged, like unto a small scimitar. Its pommel was semicircular, and both it and the hilt were of pure brass. Its quillions were a single conical piece that sloped gracefully down to the blade. The blade was broad for a dagger and was etched with blue Elvish runes on both sides. Almiras the warrior had had it forged for his son when he came of age.

Gollmorn did not give the order to attack, as he was too taken aback by this unexpected scene to take any action. He and his men simply stared in amazement at the flamboyant display, not knowing what to think.

Surgessar cried aloud: "Grimirion! Grimirion! Elsté! Elsté! Grimirion, Grimirion!"

Léofric was next to Súndéa. "Grimirion? What does that-?"

Léofric's question was cut short by an earsplitting roar from the sky. All eyes turned upward to see a great dragon with scales of fiery orange gold flying down out of the heavens. All were struck with awe, as dragons were seldom seen south of the Elvenlands in Irminsul, especially since the beginning of the war.

Before the enemy had a chance to flee, the dragon enveloped Gollmorn's infantry in a wall of flame. Men went down like stalks of wheat before the scythe, hands futilely beating at flaming mail. None escaped its deadly flame. Those who ran were soon caught by its searching beam of searing fire. Even the steam of its normal breath was hot enough to kill a man at a great distance. Gollmorn clenched his teeth and shook his fist futilely at the meddling elf magic that was destroying half of his army. The very roar of the beast seemed a mocking laugh to him.

The beast would have moved on to the cavalry. But suddenly, a carefully aimed bolt from a dying crossbowman struck it in the throat, the one vulnerable point in its scaly armor. Gollmorn breathed a sigh of relief. The dragon wheezed thunderously, and fell with a great crash. Surgessar inclined his head in a token of thanks and whispered a benediction for his slain friend.

Léofric gasped, "Why did he not summon that beast earlier, during a previous battle? It would have been a great aid to us."

"The yearly hibernation period of the Brilvarn, or benevolent fire worms of the Elvenlands, ended but a fortnight past," Súndéa whispered in reply.

"Well," mused Cynric, a bit astonished. "I have seen my first benevolent dragon today." He was surprised, for all the dragons that inhabited his icy homeland were malevolent, their ancestors having been originally placed there by the Dark Enemy to fulfill his evil purposes.

Their unexpected advantage was gone as suddenly as it had come. The cavalry of Irminsul charged forth with a cry. The forces of Gollmorn charged to meet them. In the center of the plain, they clashed in a literal explosion of steel.

Léofric was instantly caught up in the violence of the fray. Filled with the energy that only battle can bring, he slashed and hacked left and right, felling many men for a first battle. The silvered Dwarven shield that Kettil the half-Dwarven smith had given him had already deflected many blows of his enemies, yet it in no way became notched or dented. The good Dwarven steelcraft was proving its mettle in the heat of battle. The blood of the slain slipped off the star-engraved blade as if it had been wrought of otter's skin and did not stain the good steel at all.

When he had a chance to look up for a mere second, he glanced toward Súndéa, who was twirling her sickle-bladed swords skillfully and fatally, as she slashed a man across the chest. The noble battle fury of her people burned in her eyes. Nearby, her father practiced the graceful swordsmanship of the elves, swinging his scimitar in broad sweeping blows, cutting down foes at every turn, singing the songs of the deeds of Elven warriors of old. He would not be ashamed to stand among them if such were his fate that day.

High above the battle, his red-haired Elven friend flew, his horned mount snorting with battle fury. At intervals, he would swoop down, the blade of his sword singing and flashing through the air like a beam of pearl sunlight.

Randomly, he selected a lone pikemen that had miraculously survived the dragon's onslaught, though he was singed. Taking careful aim, the elf hurled his spear with all his might. It sailed down swiftly, and found its intended mark in the heart of the enemy pikeman who had somehow escaped the fiery downpour by sheer chance.

Little did the Elven general know that the man he had just slain was Jarkin, the captain whose men had caused the downfall of Halifar and his men. The rebel captain had not received the promotion he desired, for, when he was so bold as to request it, Gollmorn had flown into a rage, and had cut off the captain's thumb with his own dagger.

The elf had avenged the brave Halifar. Yet, Naemar knew not of the deed that had been wrought by his hand. The vengeance that Rothgaric had intended to take for his dear friend had been achieved by another, unknowing warrior.

Over the din of battle, Léofric heard a sound like that of the growling of a wolf mixed with the roar of a dragon. "Huum hara huum!"

Léofric turned to see Khrua-Hadrim, oblivious of his many bleeding wounds, lunging like a mad dog at his brother, Khard-Ghurad. A mad fire of vengeance and hatred burned red in the Vólderín's eyes. His primitive rage was elevated to its crescendo. His brother was armed with a blackened broadsword and wore a shirt of blackened mail. This seemed very out of place with his unkempt beard and the deerskin that he wore beneath the armor.

A long rumbling sound came from Khrua's throat, and he shouted, "Coward traitor wears hard shirt. Too afraid fight like true Vólderín. Gham hura huum!"

Khard-Ghurad was highly untrained in the art of the sword, so he easily gave way to his brother's wild, raining blows. Wielding a steel-headed warhammer was apparently easy for Khrua, as he had trained all his life with his great oaken maul, which was in truth much heavier than the single-handed hammer he now bore.

With one horizontal blow, Khrua struck his brother in the gut with the back spike of the hammer. Khard-Ghurad fell to the ground with a guttural groan, clutching his wounded stomach and dropping his sword. Something that might be called a grin crossed the other Vólderín's lips.

Khrua did not waste time with famous triumphant words, but, killing his brother with a single powerful blow to the temple, wrenched his weapon free. The other Vólderín had gone over to fight with another clan during a feud, and had betrayed his own flesh and blood, an unforgivable sin for a Vólderín. Now the chieftain's younger son had finally avenged his father's death.

"Ghan-Haradul, you are avenged," rumbled the victorious Vólderín.

For the rest of his life, Léofric was haunted in his dreams by the ghastly image of Khrua, standing victorious astride the body of his brother, his weapon red with the blood of the betrayer of his father. He was, in that moment, the colossus of savagery.

Then, a melodious yet somewhat grating song reached Léofric's ears. He turned to see Dunndag and his men, unhorsing and then killing enemy cavalrymen with their spiked mauls and axes, singing as they slew.

"Hum, hum! Axe mine!
Crush the skull, break the spine!
Mail-clad men on the forest floor,
Let us throw stones and break down the door!"

Léofric suddenly began to hear a strange thudding sound coming from the edge of the fray. He looked to see Cynric, his axes too clotted with blood to be useful anymore, using his immense strength to heft the dead horses over his head and hurl them at oncoming enemy riders.

As an enemy cavalryman charged him, the dwarf knocked him from his horse with a dead mount. The mailed man's horse lost its footing and careened into the dwarf, crushing the bearded warrior and dying upon the upturned blade of one of his axes.

Léofric forced his way to where the dwarf lay beneath the dead horse.

"Hold on, master dwarf," Léofric panted, "hold on to life."

"No. Do not worry with me, lad. The greatest honor is mine: to die in the greatest battle of the age. Cýling will be proud of his son. Alas, I cannot tell you of my many adventures, laddie." The dwarf's eyes glazed over in death.

Though he had known him for such a short time, Léofric felt a deep sadness at the dwarf's passing. He was the strongest, bravest, yet most reckless warrior the boy had ever known, and he had met many valiant warriors over the past months. Léofric longed to be told of the dwarf's many adventures in his icy homeland, but now that could never be. He was now seated at the great feast table with the five fathers of the dwarves and with his father, Cýling. He had more than once proved himself worthy of their mighty company.

Despite the skill of the warriors of Irminsul, the fight was turning in favor of the rebels. The cavalry was wavering, when suddenly, the red-bearded man saw an opening through which he could reach his enemy. It was extremely narrow, but was an opening nonetheless. Rothgaric urged his great white stallion through the fray. High above the battle, Naemar saw and understood his motive. Reigning his flying mount to hover at an angle to Rothgaric's charging horse, he whispered, "Éa ilonde."

A beam of blinding white light issued from the horn of the unicorn. The flaring white beam reflected off Rothgaric's vambraces and into the eyes of Gollmorn's bodyguards. They cried out and fell to the ground, shielding their eyes against the incredible light with their mailed hands.

Standing in the stirrups, Rothgaric hurled his massive body at Gollmorn. The force of the blow knocked the unsuspecting villain from the saddle, and the two commanders wallowed together on the ground for a moment, kicking a tattoo of grass in the air.

Struggling to their feet, they faced each other. Gollmorn was armed with a massive broadsword with an undulating blackened blade. Their swords clashed and the fury of their strokes caused sparks to fly. The two men were equally skilled with the blade, but nothing could stop the righteous fury of the red giant. Summoning all his strength, Rothgaric knocked the sword out of Gollmorn's hands. For the first time, fear crept into Gollmorn's snakelike eyes.

"May your soul crawl in the muck till the ending of the world, traitor," Rothgaric cried.

"Fool," cried the deranged commander, stepping forward and thrusting his sweaty face into Rothgaric's. He foamed at the mouth as he spoke and his eye twitched, for he was completely drunk with his dreams of glory. "You shall not judge me from the silver throne of Auraheim."

"No, I cannot judge you. Only Gildéador may truly judge the hearts and deeds of men, elves and dwarves. May He have mercy on your soul." Thus declared Rothgaric, and with one great horizontal stroke, decapitated the rebel general.

Picking up the blackened broadsword from the bloodied ground, Rothgaric sheathed his sword and blew the mighty silver war horn of Nilmeron with all the breath that was left in his weary, heaving breast. Its call was clear and commanding and was heard across the battlefield. All the fighting seemed to pause at its sounding, for almost spellbinding was its note. There stood the next King, the revitalizer of the line of the Sword Dreamers, a second Nilmeron, much loved of Gildéador, victorious, the sun brilliantly illuminating his silvered mail.

Rothgaric cried, his lungs and heaving breast filled with new strength at the sight of victory, "Gollmorn is dead. Surrender now, and you will all be spared."

Even over the expanse of the plain of battle, every one of the enemy heard the offer. There was a great clanking sound as many weapons clattered to earth.

Rothgaric walked haltingly over to Surgessar. The dark elf was sweaty and his surcoat and mail were rent in many places. "You shall send them north to your people as slaves." The elf merely nodded, too exhausted from his exertions to speak.

There arose a mighty cheer of victory and a cry of, "Hail, King Rothgaric!" The Army gathered the surrendering prisoners and then rode north to Auraheim.

On the journey, the brave, fiery-haired Naemar rode high above the Army of Irminsul on his unicorn, to make sure they reached the Silver City in safety before he departed for his homeland to report the victory to his master. As his beautiful mount's wings beat the air, he began to sing loudly.

"The war of strife is over and done,
For the hour of the Red King has come.
Spread the word, Irminsul is free
A new Nilmeron rides to the Silver City.
Faethas, Gildéador, Faethas."

As the Army of Irminsul entered Auraheim, the beat of unicorn's wings was heard to the north of the city.

SIXTEEN

ELVISH LESSONS

The Silver City of Auraheim was a large, thriving city at the base of the northern Kjartens that was protected by sturdy, rectangular walls of thick stone coated with silver. Four rectangular towers stood at each of the four corners of the wall. High above each of these towers flew a large banner of silver emblazoned with the white unicorn of Irminsul. The northern gates and southern gates were identical, each consisting of double doors built of strong oak, thirty feet high and about eight feet wide, reinforced with thick steel bars and coated from top to bottom with silver. These provided the only entrance and egress to and from the city and could only be opened using great wenches in the watchtowers above.

As the great mailed host drew near the city, the guards standing at the battlements could not see who led the approaching Army. They thought it may be a clever, deceptive device of the enemy.

A man with flowing hair as white as goose down and a short beard of the same hue appeared at the battlement above the gate as the heralds blew their great war horns. The young guard standing at the captain's side called in a voice strong: "Who approaches the Silver City of Auraheim? Are you a friend or a foe?"

Maelthaen was riding next to Rothgaric. He laughed and called up in a loud voice, "Eldénéod, my old uncle, do you not recognize your own nephew? The King has come to be crowned. The forces of Gollmorn are defeated."

The old captain laughed, his voice hoarse with tears. "I shall grant you passage into the city and more. But first, my eyes are somewhat weaker than those of the young men I command, and I would use these old eyes to see this wonder close at hand. I did not think that at seventy-eight years of age, I would be fortunate enough to live to see the war finally won."

In a moment, the great silver gates creaked open, and the elderly captain of the guard walked stiffly out to the victorious army. He stood a little above six feet in height, though he was somewhat bent by his years of service. He leaned slightly upon a long-shafted spear that he used as a walking stick, but his sword arm appeared to be still quite strong. He was clad in light mail over which he wore a long cloak of silver gray cloth which was pinned by a pearl brooch in the shape of a unicorn. On his feet he wore large silver-gray boots of dyed leather. He had become a guard of the Silver City at a young age, and had, because of his prowess and faithful service, been elevated to the captaincy.

A short but broad-bladed hand-and-a-half stabbing sword with steel fittings hung in a sheath of brown leather at his waist. The shapes of the fittings were similar to those on Rothgaric's broadsword. The grip was wrapped in rich brown leather and was inlaid with circular steel studs all along its length. It was passed from the captain of the guard to his successor.

Eldénéod inclined his head toward Rothgaric, his eyes misting anew with happy tears. He took off the sword he carried in its baldric.

He humbly spoke to Rothgaric, "My lord, I must boldly ask your indulgence. Our law decrees that, in perilous times when there is no King, the captain of the guard of the Silver City may appoint his successor himself. I seek your permission to do this."

Rothgaric smiled. "You may do so freely, my friend, for I am not yet crowned."

The old man handed the sword up to Maelthaen, saying, "My nephew, I hope you will serve this city in happier times than did your predecessor."

"Thank you, my uncle," Maelthaen said solemnly, taking the sword.

Eldénéod spoke again to Rothgaric, "Is this the Sword Dreamer of which we have heard rumors?" motioning to Léofric.

"This is he," replied Rothgaric.

The old captain then turned to Léofric. "Blessed am I to see the peace of this land restored. In all my sixty years of serving this city, I have never seen so happy an hour. The one bit of wisdom I can give you, brave young paladin, is this: though you have served her mightily, your service to the kingdom is never over. Your friends and loved ones have been instrumental in helping to bring you to this place and have helped you to accomplish your mission. Never forget those who have come alongside you to support you as you follow your calling." The gates were then opened and the victorious Army entered Auraheim.

The joyous people crowded along the main street to greet the battle-weary heroes with loud shouts of praise. Rothgaric rode at the head of the Army, and except for his fiery red beard, he had the appearance of mighty Nilmeron, returning victorious from battle against the Vólderíns in the days of old.

For three weeks, preparations for the coronation ceremony were made. During this time Rothgaric was seldom seen, leaving the administrative duties to Irphirion, the elderly keeper of the city. However, his few duties included posing for a marble statue to be erected in the marble Hall of Kings near the center of the city. Doing so made him very uncomfortable, as he was a man of war and not accustomed to such things. The poor master sculptor was even more perturbed, for Rothgaric had the physique of a bear, and was the most powerfully built man to sit on the throne of Irminsul since mighty Nilmeron in the days now long past. This made it extremely difficult for the poor sculptor to capture his likeness.

Léofric spent his time with Surgessar and learning more Elvish runes and lore. The dark elf took his leave of the Army with a sizeable pension to become the tutor of the soon-to-be High Prince. This had been arranged at Rothgaric's request.

"My old friend," Rothgaric had said when he found time to speak with the elf in private. "It is my intention that the people of the Irminsul should know more of Elven lore and wisdom. Though I have spent many years with you, I know very little of your language and history. It should not be so with my son. He must set an example to his future subjects. I would be honored if you would tutor him in the lore and language of your people. Though the blood of a fighter flows in your veins, I see that you grow weary of the Army, and would have a simple life spent in peaceful pursuits. What say you?"

"It would be an honor, my dear friend," Surgessar boomed.

When Léofric was informed of his father's plans, he was very pleased. "Perhaps you shall be teaching me the lore of your people until the end of your days," he joked happily. The lessons kept Léofric from becoming overly concerned with his mother, with whom he knew he would soon be reunited.

One day shortly thereafter, as the tall elf and his pupil walked in the Palace garden, they watched the spring lilies in bloom and followed with their eyes the path of the graceful winding ivy reaching its delicate tendrils down the silver walls. Surgessar was finishing the recitation of an Elvish lay that he had translated.

> *"And so the Vólderíns, they fell.*
> *Gladdéas was named Nilmeronel.*
> *Nilmeron laid up his war tool*
> *And ruled over Irminsul."*

"That was truly a wondrous ballad," said Léofric. "I hope that when I am King I shall be as noble and true as Nilmeron."

Surgessar smiled. "You have a heart like unto his, so that is more than possible, my friend."

"Tell me more of Gildéador, that I may honor His Name, now and when I am ruler of Irminsul."

"Ah, a perfect place to end our lessons for today. Please, sit down on that rock and be still. I must tell you of Éacané, the Song of Being. It was begun by Gildéador Himself, and is the way in which the world was created and is governed in harmony. Though the Dark Enemy sought from the beginning, and still seeks to sow discord within it, the composer and conductor of the Song was, and is, and always will be Gildéador, The King That Is. We all have a part to add to the ever-growing song, for good or ill. Halifar's part was one of the sweetest melodies I have ever heard in all of my many days. He knew very little of Gildéador or the great battle that pervades all, yet he was a flaming, resounding chorus for the good of Éacané, though he knew it not. You heard his beautiful refrain as he sang around the fire of the deeds of warriors of old. It spoke to your soul. That was what gave unspeakable joy to your heart whenever you were near him. Be still, concentrate and you shall hear the Great Symphony. Your heart is ready now."

Léofric closed his eyes tightly and concentrated. Slowly, he began to hear the sweetest melody, to which no music or singing that he had before heard even could compare, an age-old song from beyond the depths of time. At first, it was very quiet, almost indiscernible. Then it grew in volume and vigor, until it filled the boy's whole hearing, a resounding symphony of golden beauty. Every thing that was good and pure contributed a part. Léofric heard it in his very soul. Everything had its own individual tempo and melody, yet they all seemed to come together to form one harmonious, everlasting song. Léofric himself was part of it and contributed his own individual, beautiful melody. He stood up amidst the beauty of the garden and laughed aloud for joy. He had found his own niche in the Great Symphony, and it gave him great peace and deepest joy, greater than any he had ever experienced.

The next morning, Léofric waited long in the garden for Surgessar. When the dark-skinned elf still did not come after an hour of waiting, the young prince went to look for him.

Léofric found him in his apartment, standing before an opened iron-bound chest, the contents of which were spread on the dresser. Surgessar was looking at a large slab of aquamarine stone, which shimmered in the light that spilled upon it through the open window.

Coming to stand beside the dark elf, Léofric saw that upon the slab was a lion cut out of white cloth. It stood upon its hind legs and its mouth was open as if in a roar. A white scimitar blade was coming out of its mouth and a fierce look was in its eye. It looked like a coat of arms that would ride upon a battle standard.

"What is this, my friend?" Léofric asked softly, indicating the white lion.

"It is the insignia of my father," the elf answered solemnly. "Today is the anniversary of his death."

"I am sorry. Please, if it does not pain you overly much, tell me more of your father."

Surgessar drew in a deep breath. "My father, Almiras fiannathar, or 'the warrior' in the Elven language, was the greatest swordsman in all the Elvenlands. The men in the Army of Irminsul marvel at my deftness with the blade, but truly, my skill is nothing compared to that of my father. He taught Naemar and me how to wield the blade, but we could never surpass or best him. He distinguished himself in the recurring wars between my people and the invading Vólderíns. The wild men feared him and rightly so. He would charge into battle with no helmet upon his head, his dark hair braided with gold rings. He wore a shirt of silver-coated mail with the sleeves cut off, so as not to hinder the swinging of his massive arms. He was as tall as I am though he had a build more like that of your father. Near the center of the mail shirt, many rings were left white to form the insignia you see here. He chose that for his insignia because he knew that the Word of The King That Is is vibrant with life and is ever working, sharper than any physical sword.

"My father wielded two scimitar-like swords. The fittings were of silver and were inlaid with turquoise, and the grips were wrapped in silver wire. His swords flashed like bolts of silver lightning in every battle as he felled wild men left and right. He also wore breeches and boots of tough, boiled leather dyed silver-blue and laced with mail. Like him, I sing songs of the Elven warriors of old as I fight in battle.

"When he died, I did not join the Army of Nilmeronel as my blood brother Naemar did, because I knew that if I did, I would be expected to live up to my father's reputation, which I could not do. Instead I sought adventure to the south, after having this insignia removed from my surcoat, so I would not be identified and attacked by the many enemies of my father who dwelt in the northern Kjartens. That is why the blue surcoat that I have worn for years has no emblem.

"I miss my father, and I know I will see him again someday. But not yet, for I know The King That Is has not yet finished his great work in me."

He retrieved a pair of large, fingerless gauntlets from the iron-bound chest. They were made from boiled leather dyed silver-blue and were laced with strands of mail.

Handing them to Léofric, the dark elf said, "My father wore these in every battle in which he fought. They will not fit your hands now, but you would do me great honor to wear them in battle when you are King, though I pray that your reign will be one of peace."

The day after he learned of Almiras the warrior, Léofric was thinking deeply of Halifar's passing. He knew that the raven-haired captain had been a joyous, wonderful part of the Song of Being, but he could not help but wonder if he would ever see him again.

As Surgessar and the young prince walked again in the Palace garden, Léofric said, "Your people are the oldest and wisest in the world. What do elves know of what happens after death?"

"Ah," Surgessar said, his voice taking on a tone of reverence. "I must tell you of Vylcanéunon, servant of Gildéador and Walker of the Sea. When someone dies who has yielded their life to the will of The King That Is, they are taken, as if in a dream, to the shores of the Elverean Sea. There they are met by a mysterious sage. He is as tall as an elf and has our pointed ears. But his face is that of an old dwarf, wrinkled and nearly covered by a great, silky white beard. Also, he has the square cut mane and the voice of a man. In his hand he carries a tall staff wrought of pure silver, and upon his yet mighty back, he wears a robe that dances with the bright blue-green colors of the sea and upon his shoulders is draped a cloak of tattered black silk. He will lead you on a journey across the sea, clearing a path through the waves with his staff. As you walk toward the darkening horizon he shall sing the song of your life to Gildéador. That is what his name means in the Elven tongue, "The Good Singer". If The King That Is takes pleasure in the song (and if you give your life to Him, He will), you shall be taken up into the Halls of Gildéador in the sky. There you will be given a new voice with which to join with all creation in the singing of the Song of Being. Let your soul be at peace. I know why you questioned me about this, and rest assured that our friend Halifar has added his mighty new voice, even mightier than the one he possessed in life, to the Everlasting Chorus."

Léofric was comforted by what the dark elf said, and his soul was at peace, for he knew he would see his mighty friend again, after the Walker of the Sea had brought him hence when his time came.

SEVENTEEN

THE RED KING

The sisterhood of healers tended to the wounded until they were ready to be sent home. Many of the veteran soldiers decided to stay in Auraheim, however, for they wanted to see the coronation ceremony of the man who had led them valiantly for so many years. They loved him as their brother and as their master, and were willing to follow him to the death if the need arose.

The one who was most seriously wounded and received the most care was Dunndag Greenmail, the last chieftain of the Vulder-vogund rangers, for, after the battle, he found that his many wounds were deep due to the inferior quality of his mail.

Alas, he was now a chieftain without a tribe, for all his men had died in the battle, the superior weapons of the enemy easily rending through their crude hauberks. But they had fought with the ferocity of dragons, swinging up heavy, fatal blows even as they fell to their deaths.

As the Army was gathering the wounded, the realization of the death of his men struck Dunndag the ranger chieftain like a death blow from his own maul. He sank to his knees in despair, pulling at his mangy hair and wailing at the top of his lungs, in the proper manner of mourning of his now extinct people. When he finally left the battlefield, he stumbled from side to side, as if drunk, for his grief was too great for even his stout heart to bear. How he longed to share in the fate of his men, the last of the brave green-mailed Vuldervogund warriors.

News of the victory over the rebels spread from the city like a contagious disease, becoming quite jumbled once it reached the Southlands. Some said Futhark had been rejuvenated to the days of his youth. Some said a mighty Elven Prince, like unto Nilmeron in the days of old, had taken control of the city. Some said he had known what to do by looking in a crystal ball.

So it was that when Ragna was sent for by the King, she did not know the reason why or what to expect when she arrived. She had taken to wearing black for the loss of her son, whom she assumed had gone to war and had been eaten on the journey north by the great wolves in Firbolg Forest. The management of the farm had been very difficult since he disappeared, but that was the least of her sorrows.

Ragna was sitting on the stoop before the house, half-mindedly weaving a basket out of twine and thinking despairingly of her lost son, when she heard the trot of horses. Looking up, she was astonished to see a great silver carriage drawn by a team of four white stallions coming swiftly toward the house, followed by a silver stall drawn by a team of six stallions of the same white color. There were four mail-clad riders riding before and behind the carriage, each bearing the unicorn banner of Irminsul.

The sides of the sparkling carriage as well as its door were painted with swirling white designs, over which the pearl-white unicorn was prominent. The wheels were rimmed with shining steel and shone in the morning sunlight. The cushions were of fluffy white fur filled with goose down. On the back running board stood a mail-clad man with a flaxen mane, apparently the leader. He raised his hand in greeting as the carriage slowed to a halt before her.

Not knowing what to think, she grabbed the wooden pitchfork that was leaning against the wall, to defend herself in case these men meant her ill. The people of the Southlands were suspicious of soldiers from the northern cities. One of her first inclinations was to run away, but that would leave her home defenseless.

"Good morrow," said the man in a stoic tone. "You are Ragna, daughter of Baelbor the weaver?"

"I am," she answered softly, tightening her grip on the pitchfork and poising to flee. "What do you want of me?"

"The King has sent for you and wishes you to come to Auraheim."

"What should the King want with me? We care little for him in these parts. He knows that."

"My orders are to bring you back. You must come with us."

"How can I trust you? How do I know you will not just loot my house and burn it to the ground? Did the men from The Red Griffin tell you I would be easy prey?"

The blond man cast up his eyes in frustration and drew his sword. "I, Maelthaen, son of Dragohir, swear upon this blade and upon my honor as a captain in the Army of Irminsul, and on my honor as the new captain of the guard of the Silver City that you will not be harmed."

Ragna slowly released her hold on the pitchfork and walked cautiously forward, hesitantly allowing one of the riders to help her up into the fine carriage. She still did not know what to think of it all, and was, in truth, very frightened.

"My orders are also to bring your milk cow. It is strange, but the King requested it."

The escort party would say nothing of their purpose on the journey to the Silver City. Therefore, she had no idea of the surprise that would await her in Auraheim. The carriage arrived at the Royal Palace in the late afternoon of the day before the coronation ceremony. Rothgaric had asked that none of the citizens be there to greet their Queen, though some of them could not help looking out their windows at the comical sight of a dun cow from the Southlands being brought up before the Palace. Rothgaric was not wearing the diadem or mail of the King at the time, but was clothed in a rich red jerkin and cape lined with gray fur, and trousers of dark wool.

The footman helped her out and Rothgaric ran to meet her, while Léofric waited atop the steps. Barely glancing at the man in the red jerkin and cape coming to meet her, her eyes locked onto the familiar face of her son. Ragna's heart leapt in her chest, as she pushed her way past the mail-clad guards and sprinted to Léofric, taking no notice of the red-bearded man.

She embraced him tightly and her many tears soon stained his surcoat. "Oh, my son. Thank heaven. I took you for dead. I thought you had abandoned me. What is this? Armor? Why are you in this strange place? What are you doing here?"

Léofric embraced her tightly for a moment and then pushed her gently away. Pointing back over her shoulder, he quietly intoned, "Father". Ragna turned. Only then did she see the handsome red-haired warrior who was standing a few paces behind her. When he held out his hand to her she froze, her visage nearly expressionless. Slowly, recognition dawned on her tear-streaked face. Her eyes widened disbelievingly and her jaw dropped. She pointed at him, but no words came.

Finally, she cried, "Rothgaric! Is it truly you? You abandoned me for all those years. I labor at backbreaking work with a tiny babe in my arms. Everyone looks down on me. My own father disowns me for shame. I raise our son for almost twenty years. I do not know if you are alive or dead and now you…Why?" She turned to Léofric and burst into tears anew, seeming as if she would swoon.

Rothgaric took her by the hand and led her into the palace. Turning back to Léofric, he said, "Son, leave us. Your mother and I have much of which to speak together." Then he led her through the great silver doors to the royal apartments.

The lamps burned low in the private chamber of the King, and their voices were heard in earnest conversation late into the night. By the next morning, Ragna had regained her cheerful demeanor and was in the highest of spirits, such as Léofric had never seen her in before. It gave his heart great joy to see her so heartened. He embraced her often and delighted in describing his gift as the Sword Dreamer to her, and telling her of his many adventures. She was also very pleased when she met Súndéa, and could discern, through the intuition that only a mother can possess, that her son cared for her very much. She often praised him for all the wonderful deeds that he had done during the war as her motherly pride sparkled in her eyes.

"I am proud of you my son," she said with tears in her eyes. "You have been used mightily for the good of all, and have been blessed beyond my greatest imagination. Now, because of your courage and perseverance, your father and I can renew our vows of marriage. I shall help your father rule, true, but it was through you that all this has been made possible."

That morning at the breakfast table in the great personal dining hall of the King, Rothgaric sent the servers away, cleared his throat and stood up. He was dressed in a red velvet jerkin accompanied by a red cape of the same material. The cape was lined with rich grey wolf fur. "My love," he said, sounding somewhat unsure of himself. "During the time I was waiting for you to arrive, Surgessar assisted me in composing a ballad expressing my love for you. I am neither a poet nor a minstrel, but a simple man. The Elvish terms do not come easily to my tongue." He produced a piece of parchment, and once again cleared his throat. He then began singing in a clear, steady voice. It was the same tune as that of the ballad that Nilmeron had composed for Luaria on their wedding day long ago.

"Thy love has returned to thee,
Clada Irminsularion.
For thee I would cross the Elverean Sea,
Rhionna Aelgaelbrystarion.
Come dwell forever in my hall
Clada Nilmarion.
There shall be love, peace and all,
Clada Aelgaelbrystarion.

Léofric looked over at his mother, and saw tears running down her cheeks, her deep joy written on her beaming, smiling face. Her heart overflowed with the deepest love for Rothgaric. She and her husband were bound by a bond of love that no hardship or war could cut asunder.

Léofric finally had been blessed with that which his heart had secretly longed for all his life: a reunited family bound by the unbreakable bonds of Gildéador's everlasting love. The hope that he had not allowed to die had been fed by the love of his mother. Faith in the faithfulness of his father had blossomed once he had let go of all the years of pain. Truly, hope, love and faith were Gildéador's greatest and most imperishable gifts to all his children. At that moment, Léofric's soul dwelled in the richness of these priceless gifts, and he silently laughed for joy. The King That Is had generously poured great blessings into the Sword Dreamer's life, and for that Léofric, son of Rothgaric, was truly thankful.

Luath was put in the King's silver stable, and was fed from a silver feeding trough. Thus Léofric's dream came true. While his father was in revealing the secrets of the past to Ragna, Léofric took Súndéa to visit the dun cow in her new abode.

As he stroked her hide, Léofric whispered in Luath's ear. "This is the girl I beheld in my dreams. All the hopes and dreams I told you of have come to pass, my old friend. If you yield your life to The King That Is and surrender yourself to His will, He will give you the desires of your heart."

Léofric continued to milk Luath for the rest of her days, for even a prince must be a servant. She provided the best milk, butter and cheese for the King's table and was the most beloved cow in all of Irminsul.

Éalrohil, golden lord of Nilmeronel, one of the most powerful princes of the Elvenlands, had come with a following at the request of Surgessar. He was the tallest elf Léofric had ever seen, standing almost seven and a half feet. His pale skin was shining like alabaster and his flaxen tresses were almost golden in hue. His light blue eyes resembled precious aquamarine crystals and bespoke the great wisdom commonly found in the elder children of Gildéador. It was to him that Rothgaric had sent the rebels. This, the King hoped, would renew commerce and strengthen the good will between Irminsul and the Elvenlands, for all trade and travel between Irminsul and Nilmeronel had ceased during the war.

The morning before the coronation, before the coach bearing Léofric's mother had arrived, Éalrohil had come to Rothgaric, accompanied by his mighty sons, the Princes Cluadrimril and Cludaeron. Their hair was as golden as their father's and they were nearly as tall as he. The Elven brothers did not speak human speech, having never journeyed outside of Nilmeronel, and they only saluted silently as they entered. The towering Elven lord of Nilmeronel was clad in a mail coat whose rings were as white as freshly fallen snow. Only the Elven smiths of Nilmeronel knew the secret of how to forge mail of that color. They used the soft petals of the beautiful soft Galifas flower, which was native to Nilmeronel and after which Éalrohil's father had been named, to provide the armor with a brilliant white sheen. Over the hauberk, the elf lord wore a wine red surcoat emblazoned with the golden shield of Nilmeronel. He also wore steel vambraces on his wrists which were smelted over with gold. Upon his head rode a round golden diadem about an inch thick. In the center of the diadem was an emerald that sparkled so brightly it seemed almost to blaze with green fire. At his waist he carried a slender broadsword in a wine red leather sheath with gold furniture. The fittings were also of gold and the elm wood grip was wrapped with silver wire. This was the sword of Laeglam. Its blade was of pure white steel, and it had been passed down from princely father to son since the days of Laeglam's battles against the Dark Enemy in the days when the world was young.

The Elven lord's sons were similarly dressed, though they wore no crowns. Each Prince bore a great two-handed ceremonial broadsword and a huge buckler of whitened steel in a silver baldric on his back.

Éalrohil inclined his head in greeting, and said, "You have proven your mettle against almost insurmountable odds. Even when I could not help you, you fought to defend your people against the shadow of tyranny that long loomed menacingly over them. For that, you have my deepest respect. You led your forces with compassion and wisdom, with high esteem for the lives of friend and enemy alike. You are ready to rule, Rothgaric Elf-friend. Henceforth, you shall be known in my land as Gilda Aelgaelbryst, King Fire Beard, and bear the honorary title of Eldag-eileanne, Elf-friend. You have proven yourself worthy to be King of Irminsul, as your predecessor, Nilmeron proved himself of old by defending the land he had sworn to protect. I am proud to call myself your ally, though the bonds of kinship by blood between my realm and yours were broken with the passing of King Futhark. We are not related by blood, but we have a kinship in our hearts through The King That Is, the likes of which can never be broken."

After saying these words, Éalrohil produced a small object wrapped in a white linen cloth, and handed it to Rothgaric. Inside was a large brooch replication of the golden shield of Frékanéor that rode proudly on the standard of Nilmeronel. It had a small emerald for the central boss. This was the standard of the Army of Nilmeronel and the coat of arms of the House of Frékanéor, for it was the golden shield that Laeglam had had forged for his son Frékanéor after Frékanéor returned with the tamed stallion, Maelros.

"General Naemar wished for me to give you this as a token of his gratitude for letting him fight in battle with you and your men. I do not begrudge him for making that choice. Rather, I gave him my blessing, for I myself would have fought with you, at the head of a body of five thousand heavily armed Elven horsemen, had I but been able. All the captains in my Army have a brooch such as this which they wear into battle. Wear it with pride, my brother. I will entreat Gildéador that it will never see use during your long reign. May it be one of peace and prosperity. Maegaelannin: May the days of the King of Irminsul be blessed always by The King That Is."

Rothgaric then gave back to the Elven Prince the silver-hilted sword of Nilmeron that had served for all the days of the House of Nilmeron as the sword of the King of Irminsul. Its blade was broad and forged of the finest steel. Its hilt was of pure silver and it could be wielded with one or two hands. Its guard was long and thick and its pommel was semicircular. The entire length of the sword, from the pommel to the tip of the blade was inscribed in Elvish runes that read: "I am the sword of Nilmeron. I was forged to serve a ruler."

When Éalrohil took the weapon, his eyes began to mist with tears. It had been over a thousand years since an elf had held the sword of Nilmeron. He lifted it high above his head and the blade flashed in the morning sunlight. The elves of Nilmeronel once again had possession of both the silver-hilted sword of Nilmeron and the golden shield of Frékanéor.

The golden elf lord turned to one of his sons and softly commanded, "Cludaeron, cludathas."

The Elven prince obediently handed his father the great ceremonial sword he wore. Éalrohil placed the sword of Nilmeron into the empty silver baldric on his son's back, and gave the great sword to Rothgaric. "Faethas," said he. "One good blade deserves another, Brother Aelgaelbryst."

Éalrohil then took his leave, saying, "Farewell, King Rothgaric Aelgaelbryst, he who has the courageous heart of a wolf."

After the audience with the Elven lord, Rothgaric had prepared for the arrival of the carriage bearing his long-estranged wife and soon to be Queen.

In the afternoon of the day before the coronation, Kettil the old weapon smith came to see Léofric, now proclaimed as the High Prince of Irminsul. The mighty half dwarf bore with him something wrapped in a dark blue cloth. The old smith had dressed in his best for the occasion. He had, that morning, washed off the grime and sweat of the forge and now wore a dark blue tunic and a cloak of the same color lined with gray fur. On his hands he wore gloves of black leather. He had inherited these princely garments from his father, so they fit very tightly. He seemed a bit restless, as he was unaccustomed to the finery of the Palace and the tightness of his rich Dwarven clothes did little to help his feeling of nervousness. He knelt before Léofric and put the blue cloth in his lap.

"Please unwrap this, my prince," he said as formally as he could. "It is my gift to you, in honor of your recent recognition."

Wrapped inside the cloth was the prized blue Elven blade of Aelgaelisel, Kettil's most costly possession.

"I thought it a fitting gift for the High Prince and Sword Dreamer," the old smith said, smiling.

Léofric felt his eyes misting with tears. "I thank you, my friend. From the bottom of my heart, I thank you." He handed it to Súndéa, who was seated next to him.

Kettil smiled at the ebon-skinned elf girl and, clapping his hands once, turned to see one of his assistants enter the room, a large satchel on his shoulder. Placing the pack down at his master's feet, the young man nodded respectfully and left.

"My lady Súndéa," Kettil said briskly, "I noticed that your brigandine fared badly in the battle. In this time of peace, I pray you never have to go to battle, but should the need arise..." he reached into the bundle, "I have made this for you."

He produced a brigandine of white Elven mail and soft but tough leather of a strangely magnificent quality. The material shone a brilliant orange gold, and the afternoon sun seemed to set it inwardly ablaze with an ancient, almost righteous fire, as if it had been burnished for a millennium. Attached to the shoulders were spaulders of the same fiery leather. Several pearl-white spikes of an ivory-like texture stabbed upwards from the elegant shoulder guards.

Súndéa looked at the smith curiously. "Wherever did you get the materials to make such a masterpiece?"

Kettil smiled sheepishly. "The mail was a gift from the Elven lord. The leather and spikes? Ah.... Let us just say they are a posthumous gift from a noble friend of your father's."

Súndéa nodded, comprehending. Later, she named her new brigandine Brilvarn- Lúirech: Dragon-Mail.

Rothgaric smiled at Kettil and said, "From this day forth, you, Kettil, son of Fréawulf, and all your descendents after you shall be the armorers of my House. Be watchful and ready, for I may have a unique task for you, a task concerning one of your father's countrymen. Be at peace, noble, kindhearted Kettil."

Léofric was exceedingly glad and called the good Elvish blade Gormithníl, which meant "Blue Hammer" in the ancient Elvish language.

The next day at noon, the bells of the watchtowers rang out joyously. The healers of the city had spread lilies and other sweet-smelling flowers in the fountains and on the streets so that even the very smell of the air seemed to commemorate the joyous occasion on the morning of Rothgaric's coronation.

At the appointed time, Irphirion led Rothgaric, Ragna and Léofric out in front of the Palace before the assembly of all the citizens of the city. A great cheer arose as the people saw them. The citizens were all dressed in their best to greet their new King, in a motley array of colors, such that even the poorest cloth among them seemed the richest finery in the brilliant sunlight.

No one in the entire assembly could match the splendor of the elves of Nilmeronel in the company of Éalrohil. They were a billowing sea of white, red and silver. Tall standard bearers, both light and ebon-skinned, stood in shining white mail and white surcoats, bearing the golden shield banner of Nilmeronel on tall, silver-shafted spears. The retainers of the golden Elven lord all wore ceremonial broadswords on their backs and were clad, like the standard bearers, in shining white mail. Éalrohil, his wife, the beautiful raven-haired Elven Princess Iselienin, his two sons and all of the members of his household were clad in rich red velvet to denote their rank. All of the golden Elven lord's immediate relations stood over seven feet in height. The citizens that stood around the raised platform designated to the elves were awed by their noble appearance.

The tall Elven princess wore a crown of Galifas flowers that seemed like great stars nestled in the sky of her midnight hair. Her name meant "Lady of the Autumn" in the ancient tongue of the elves, for it was a great joy to her to dance with her husband on the early evenings of fall upon the green sward of Nilmeronel's forests, when the leaves were changing to vibrant colors, but the air still clung to the warmth of the recently passed summer. Her long flowing dancing dresses would mirror the many colors of the changing leaves in many different brilliant shades of orange, red, and yellow.

The elves of Nilmeronel had been given a place of honor among the crowd and stood in the center of the assembly upon a raised marble platform. Surgessar, Súndéa and Naemar, as the Elven heroes of the final battle of the war, stood foremost among them.

Rothgaric was clad in the silvered mail of the King and still bore his old battle-weary broadsword on his back. Ragna was draped in a flowing, lily white dress laced with thread of silver. In that hour, she seemed almost restored to the full beauty of her youth. Léofric was standing to to side, dressed in the mail he had worn so often, which had been polished of blemishes once the Army had entered the Silver City. Over this he wore a silver surcoat emblazoned with the white unicorn of Irminsul.

Taking a silver goblet from a dais nearby, Irphirion gave it to them, saying, "Drink, and become united till death." It was a great joy to both of them to renew their commitment and bonds of love to each other, having been separated for so many years.

They each drank in their turn. Then he kissed her with the love and passion of one who has waited a lifetime to be with the one dearest to him.

Then, taking the silver circlet of the King from another dais, Irphirion said, "Kneel, Rothgaric of Irminsul."

Rothgaric knelt. Placing the circlet upon his head, Irphirion said, "Rise, Rothgaric, King of Irminsul."

Rothgaric rose. The people began to cheer, but he silenced them with a wave of his hand. "People of Irminsul. Today I am crowned, but the credit of the victory is not due me but rather to my son, Léofric. Hail, Léofric, High Prince of Irminsul, greatest of the Sword Dreamers." Then there arose a great cheer.

When it had subsided, Rothgaric spoke again. "Today I begin a new line of rulers. It shall be called the House of Wulf, for that was the name I used when in disguise in the Southlands on my journey to find the Sword Dreamer." Drawing his sword, he said, "This plain, simple broadsword shall be the sword of that House, now and forever. Léofric should be honored, yes, but we must give the glory of the victory to Gildéador, The King That Is, for both the battle and the victory always belong to Him. His Name shall be praised by men once again."

There arose another great cheer. After it had abated, something unexpected happened. The elves suddenly burst into song, a beautiful, harmonious mixture of Elvish and human speech.

"Hail to the King of Irminsul!
Elsté, Gilda Irminsularion!
Hail to the king, hail!
Elsté, Gilda, Elsté!

Hail to the Queen of Irminsul!

Elsté, Clada Irminsularion!

Hail to the Queen, hail!

Elsté, Clada, Elsté!

Hail Léofric, High Prince of Irminsul!

Elsté, Léofric, Laetha Irminsularion!

Hail, Sword Dreamer, hail!

Elsté, Cludalathon, Elsté!

Léofric was so overwhelmed by such wondrous praise to his name, he did not know what to think. He knew in his heart that his ears had never before heard anything so glorious.

He had one errand to do before the ceremony could progress further. He walked down the steps to the front of the crowd, bearing Halifar's sturdy long-shafted axe. There he found Wéolthea, Halifar's widow, with her son, Wéostan. They had been given that place of honor because of Halifar's faithful service. They would be cared for from Halifar's pension, which had recently been increased greatly because of his noble service to his country. Léofric handed the axe to Wéostan, saying, "Your father, the most valiant of all the soldiers of the Army of Irminsul, willed for you to bear this after him." A lump rose in Léofric's throat as he said this. The pain of Halifar's passing was still burning in his heart.

Halifar's little raven-haired son struggled to lift the weapon. Léofric laid a loving hand on his head and said, "Someday, you will be strong enough to wield it." Then he returned to stand by his father atop the Palace steps.

Khrua-Hadrim, his clothes still dirty from battle, lumbered up the steps of the Palace and knelt before Rothgaric. He was a barbarian and did not care for the finery of the city. Seeing all the guards in mail and the nobles of the city in their fine raiment made him uneasy.

Proffering his hammer, he said, "Red King Hammerfist has given Khrua vengeance. For that, Khrua grateful. Khrua's tribe always fight for Red King Hammerfist if needed. Always live in peace with shining city."

Rothgaric inclined his head in token of thanks. "I and all those who follow after me shall remember your service and live in peace with your people. Show them the steel-headed hammer I gave you as a token of my friendship. We shall always value your alliance, my friend. Go in peace."

Khrua pounded his chest twice with his fist in the manner of a salute. "Red King Hammerfist true friend of Khrua." Then he returned to the Kjarten Mountains and was never seen again in Auraheim. Rothgaric and he had a friendship and a respect that only friends that have once been enemies can have for one another: the friendship and respect of fighting men.

Surprisingly, Dunndag Greenmail the ranger chieftain did not go with Khrua, as Khrua had taken his vengeance and Dunndag's promise of aid was fulfilled. Rather, the mountain ranger stayed in the Silver City to learn his letters so that he could record the tales of the origins, deeds and wanderings of his people, that they would not die with him, the last of the wandering Vuldervogund.

Once the Vólderín had left, Rothgaric declared, "My first act as King is to commission a statue of Cynric Cýling's son, brave warrior of the Dwarvenlands, to be erected in the main square of the city. His sacrifice is a reminder to us that all the children of Gildéador, be they direct descendents or adopted, are united in a common cause against the forces of evil. Today, let us celebrate. But let us also mourn and remember those who fell, fighting valiantly in the struggle. They shall be remembered and honored in our songs and tales from this day forth. Let no generation that is to come forget the great sacrifices they made in the name of all the free peoples of Éalindé."

Kettil the sword smith had been given the blue hauberk and silvered helm of the dwarf, to melt down to provide the statue with a noble, rich outer coating. The shafts of the dwarf's bearded axes would be smelted over with silver and the weapons placed in the hands of the statue so that all could remember his brave sacrifice and future generations could be taught of the noble courage of the golden-bearded dwarf, Cynric Cýling's son, valiant slayer of Framgar the snow troll.

The coronation feast was held in the great hall of the Palace. Every citizen of the city was invited, no matter their station. Many oaken tables spread with silver cloths were laden with platters of wild fowl, mutton, pork, and many other meats, along with sweet meats, fruits and vegetables, and many sweet-tasting delicacies. In the spaces between tables, minstrels and troubadours, both human and elf kind, played music sang the songs of great heroes and their mighty deeds of old. Léofric's heart was touched again by a tinge of sadness as he thought how his friend Halifar would have enjoyed listening to the many ballads. He said a prayer of thanks to The King That Is for the blessing of Halifar's friendship and resolved to drink a toast to his memory. His only regret was that, because of his unthinkable folly before Halifar's last stand, the friendship had been ephemeral. But, as the dark elf had said, Halifar had been a vibrant, beautiful melody for Gildéador and the Song of Being.

Léofric hoped that his part in the Great Symphony would be exactly what The King That Is intended it to be, as it had been with Halifar.

The newly crowned King sat at the head of the foremost table, the unicorn banner of Irminsul above his head, reflecting the light of the many tapers on its silvery field. On either side of him sat his Queen and his son. Surgessar wore the white mail of his people over which he wore a white surcoat emblazoned with the golden shield of Nilmeronel. On his head he wore a visorless sallet, identical to the one his friend and the brother of his heart, Naemar, had worn in battle, except that this one was smelted over with white gold. It was a gift of Prince Éalrohil, taken from his own personal armory. The other captains of the Army also sat at the head table in gleaming mail of Irminsul steel. Kirlúnd still wore his prized fur cape. A fresh scar was under his left eye, a grim reminder of the final battle. The graying commander had given cautious counsel in months past, but when the time came to stand firm in the final battle, he had been as adamant as the heartiest young soldier.

The King was served first and, acting as Lord of the Feast, began eating. Everyone else followed suit once he had begun. The good wine of the Palace flowed like a river from the silvered tuns set up against the wall as the servers refilled the silver goblets again and again.

Léofric had never before in his life tasted such delicacies and was soon enjoying himself thoroughly. He suddenly looked up from his plate to see Súndéa weeping, a wistful look in her eyes. She was wearing a beautiful burgundy gown with leaves of silver cloth sewn on the billowing sleeves. It had been her mother's marriage dress, the only possession of her mother's her father had kept. It was the finest raiment she owned and contrasted sharply with her cheerless mood. He wondered how she could be so heavy of heart in this happy hour. He longed to see her comforted, for he could not bear to see her grieved.

He got up from the table and walked over to the corner where she was standing.

"What ails you, my lady?"

"Now that you are the High Prince of Irminsul, I know not what I will do. I love you, but surely a commoner and foreigner such as myself can never marry the High Prince."

Raising a finger to her lips, he said, "I swear to you, the line of the half-Elven Kings of Irminsul shall be renewed."

He took her by the hand and led her to sit next to him at the royal table.

GLOSSARY OF TERMS

AVENTAIL - long skirting of mail that falls down from the bottom of the back of the helmet to the nape of the neck to protect the back of the neck

BALDRIC - a sling for carrying a sword worn across the back or around the waist

BARBUTE – a bullet-shaped open-faced helm with a heart-shaped opening for the face

BOSS – a metal dome in the center of a shield

BRIGANDINE – a long shirt of cloth or leather sewn with ring armor (mail) or small metal plates

BUCKLER – a circular shield with a large central boss

COIF - hood of chain mail, can be worn under a helmet or alone

CROSSBOW-a bow mounted on a stock that shoots projectiles, which are often called bolts or quarrels

FALCHION - a broad sword with a curved blade

FITTINGS-comprising both the pommel and guard

FULLER(ed) - a groove running down the middle of the blade's side

GAUNTLETS - metal or leather gloves to protect the hands in battle

GORGET – a neck and clavicle guard that slips over head and is usually made of steel but possibly of leather

GREAVES - Ankle and shin guards, normally made of heavy leather and may include metal

GRIP - the handle of a sword

GUARD - the bar or other metal piece that separates the grip from the blade and provides protection for the wielder's hand

HAND-AND-A HALF SWORD – a sword that can be held with either one or two hands

HAUBERK - a long coat of chain mail armor

HELM - helmet

HILT - the entire unit of the pommel, the grip and the guard

KETTLE HELMET – a steel cap encircled by broad steel rim

LONGBOW – a very tall, sturdy bow able to shoot great distances

MACE – a spiked metal club that may have a solid handle or be connected to a handle with a chain, the length of which may be very short or quite long

MAUL - massive and very heavy hammer used in battle, often made of wood and may have steel bands or reinforcing

Nasal - the nose guard on a helmet that does not have a visor

PIKE – a pointed blade on a pole that is often used to unhorse cavalry by wedging the blunt end in the ground and pointing the blade at the underside of the charging horse

POMMEL - the cap at the top of a sword handle

QUILLION – either of the two sides of the guard

SALLET - steel helmet that slopes down a short length in the back from the head to the top of the neck for better protection of the neck area

SCABBARD/SHEATH - a case made for a sword or dagger

SCABBARD FURNITURE - metal accents at the top and bottom of a scabbard

SPAULDERS - shoulder guards, normally made of heavy leather

STEEL CAP – a plain, round steel helmet fit closely to the head

VAMBRACES - wrist guards, normally made of heavy leather

ALSO BY MARSHAL MYERS

LADY OF NAOFATIR

Miriam O'Connor is a young Victorian Irish school teacher with an avaricious love for reading and mythology. She is overjoyed when she inherits a mansion in northern England filled with a treasure trove of mythological texts. What she truly desires, however, is to find a man like those in the old stories, who will love her truly and defend her honor. One day while reading in the attic of the library, she finds an old book filled with cryptic writing. When she opens it, it whisks her off to the beautiful golden green country of Naofatir, where the fairylike inhabitants are caught in a battle against their terrible Enemy, the Dorchadas. There, she meets the Great Prince of Naofatir, and comes to discover how she can play a part in helping him save the beautiful land from destruction.

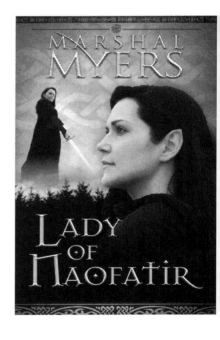